T0147566

Amy's Nightmare

Nancee Gray

iUniverse, Inc.
New York   Bloomington

iUniverse books may be ordered through booksellers or by contacting:

iUniverse
1663 Liberty Drive
Bloomington, IN 47403
www.iuniverse.com
1-800-Authors (1-800-288-4677)

ISBN: 978-1-4401-2784-7 (pbk)
ISBN: 978-1-4401-2785-4 (ebk)

Printed in the United States of America

iUniverse rev. date: 3/11/2009

Chapter 1

I never thought that I would feel the way I do, but my whole life has been changed just for the love of a man.

First, being up rooted from my family and friends and moved out of state to live at Jonathan's family country estate. Georgia is a long way from New York.

When I first saw this old house, I felt like I was being taken back in time, to an era that I didn't belong in. Then getting the sense of terrible uneasiness coming over me as we drove up the long gravel tree lined driveway. I got this feeling which I couldn't explain and have never felt before as shivers went up and down my spine.

The house, like in many old houses in horror stories I have seen, "was looking at me." Walking up on the huge verandah, I felt as if someone was taking all the breath out of my body, the feeling got worse when I touched the door knob. A hundred little electric shocks all at one time went into my fingers and up my arms. As I stood there holding the handle, the things that flashed before my eyes were enough to scare even the most hard core psychic and/or ghost chaser out of a year's growth and left me feeling dizzy when I finally let go. The bad part about it was that they flashed by me so fast that I couldn't grasp the meaning of any of them. Then within seconds they were gone and I couldn't remember any of them.

Ever since we moved into this old house, I have had this strange feeling that we should not be here and that we are not alone. Strange things happen when Jonathan is either out of the room or not at home and I'm alone, that I just passed off as my imagination playing tricks on me. I didn't know it at the time but how wrong I was.

On this dark, dreary and windy summer night I sit alone in front of the picture window in the downstairs parlor, watching for a car and/or waiting for the phone to ring. I thank God I had Jonathan install the phone when we first moved in or I'd really be lost to the outside world.

I have this feeling that there is something wrong because every time I look out the window I get this cold chill that chills me to the bone. All I need now is for it to start raining.

This feeling I have, is kind of like you know something is going to happen but you just don't know what it is or when it will happen. Usually when I get these feelings, they are right.

I have been waiting for Jonathan to come back home for what seems like hours. He stormed out of the house after that awful fight we had. Oh, how I wish hadn't said the things I said. I can't help it, but I feel that this old house is evil! I couldn't stop myself when I said this old house is haunted, but I blurted it out and wish now I hadn't. But when he said, I was just making things up, I'm a big baby, a spoiled brat, all I want is to move back to the city and that I didn't care about his feelings or his future. I couldn't help myself but lash out at him and tell him I wanted him to leave me alone. I never realized he would.

There have been weird things happening ever since we moved in, things like doors opening and closing by themselves, lights going on and off by themselves, several times the water in the kitchen would turn on, run for a while and then shut off when nobody was in the kitchen, the dishes would rattle in the cupboards. I have seen dark shadows going in and out of the upstairs rooms. I have even heard heavy footsteps coming up the stairs from the cellar when I was the only one home on day. There are times when I look into mirrors in different rooms when I think I seem an image of a woman standing behind me but when I turn around there isn't anybody there. Then there are those eyes, glowing red looking in through the windows at night. On several occasions I have seen what appears to be a dark shadow of what looks like a man pacing on the front verandah, but when I go out there to check, there isn't anybody there. But there is an unexplainable cold spot on the verandah, even on very hot days. Unfortunately these things only happen when Jonathan isn't around.

Jonathan loves this old house, it has been in his family for generations. It was once a thriving plantation. He said that I would have loved his grandmother. His grandmother was such a wonderful, wise and fun woman he says. He and his family spent many wonderful summers and holidays here when he was growing up. But things changed after his grandfather was mysteriously killed. His grandmother changed, she never wanted to talk about his grandfather, not even to his son. She became distant and somewhat of a recluse. She stopped going into town, stopped wanting to have anybody to come visit her. She didn't want anybody to be here to take care of her not even when she became so gravely ill. It was as if she lost her will to live. She died of a broken heart as they called it because they couldn't find a real reason for her death.

She told her doctors that there was something trying to kill her but the nurses, who stayed here with her, said that nobody ever came to visit her. The nurses never experienced anything out of the ordinary when she was here. Jonathan's grandmother had the look of being scared to death on her face when she died. The mortician tried to remove it but couldn't remove it completely. It looked like she had been scared to death.

Why did she leave this place to Jonathan? Why couldn't she have left it to his brother, the historical society, to charity or just sold it off? Why do I feel that there is some evil presence living in this house? Maybe that's why I think I hear sounds coming from several of the rooms upstairs. Jonathan says it's just the wind.

"This is an old house you know. Old houses creak, moan and groan. It's just settling." He would say each time I tried to get him to listen to the sounds.

But after 100 years you'd think that the house would have settled by now.

I have this feeling that something horrible happened in the master bedroom at one time. Sometimes, I feel that there is someone or something in the room with me, because I feel as if someone is watching me. I often smell cigar smoke in the bedroom. Neither Jonathan nor I smoke, but I smell it sometimes in the bedroom and sometimes in the front parlor downstairs. One time I was sitting at my dressing table, which was Jonathan's great-grandmother Angela's, I saw a woman's reflection behind me in the mirror but when I turned around there was nothing. I have felt someone touch my hair when I sitting at the dressing table. I have even heard what I thought to be voices whispering when I'm alone in some of the upstairs rooms. Every once in a while there is this sweet smell of perfume in the air in the house. It is not the kind I wear.

In the kitchen, I smell food cooking when there isn't I hear the sound of laughter which sound like children playing. One time I was in the kitchen and I heard a small voice say "Mamma." We don't have any children so it was really eerie to hear a child's voice. I have often wondered if the voices could be the children of the slaves that once worked in this old house or maybe they could be Jonathan's great-grandmother children. He was told that she had three boys and a girl, but was never

told what happened to them. I wondered if someone died in this house?

Now I sit here in the dark waiting and wondering, why doesn't he call?

I have to try to get my mind off my feeling of dread but I can't shake it. I wish that we lived closer to town or to a neighbor. I'm all alone in this huge house. I wish that Jonathan would agree to getting a dog, maybe if I had a dog it could protect me from whatever this is. I know that dog's sense things that people don't.

I loved living in our condo in the city. All our friends would come over and we would have barbeques, dinner parties, pool parties and such. It was great watching their kids for them when they would go out in the evenings. Oh, those were the days. Maybe I can find a neighbor and make friends with them.

Or, maybe a neighbor would know what happened in this house and tell me all about it. I'll have to look into that.

After Jonathan's grandmother died, her will stated that in order for Jonathan to get his inheritance, he had to live here. The Will never stated really what the inheritance was but it did say that he would come into it. Even the lawyer was puzzled by the mystery of this. He has this old locked box and the Will stated that when Jonathan turned 30 that a family member would have the key and would open it, then and only then. We only have a year to wait to find out what it is. I don't know if I can live here for a year but I'll have to try for Jonathan's sake.

During the day it has not been too bad. I finally built up enough courage to explore this old antebellum mansion. It has six soaring fluted columns with a huge verandah out front. The house has a basement that is almost the full size of the underside of the house, four stories which include a very large attic, there are 15 guest rooms, the master bedroom suite and servant's quarter's house out back, the front gate to the driveway has two huge stone lions overlooking the estate. Some of the rooms have hidden rooms behind mirrors, swiveling bookcases and behind some of the mirrors open up to secret passageways behind the walls. I am not courageous enough to explore the passageways yet but someday when I'm not alone I'll have to explore them. I wonder if there are things hidden inside the walls, such as a hidden safe, a treasure map, a secret family journal or maybe a confession note to some murder or something exciting like that.

Jonathan said that his grandmother told him that the house was built by his great, great-grandfather and each family that have lived here has added onto the house. I know that several of his ancestors have died here because the "Chamberlain" family cemetery is out in the back of the house. I wonder if any of them died inside this house or somewhere on the grounds. Maybe their restless spirits are what I am hearing and seeing. Every time I think about it I get cold shivers up and down my spine. None of Jonathan's family that we know wants to talk much about the ancestors, the house or the cemetery. That is very puzzling to me, because I had a happy childhood and everybody in my family talks about everybody and everything that ever happened. Sometimes they talk too much.

I spent one afternoon walking around in the cemetery fascinated by looking at all the names and old dates there. The creative headstones are wonderful to look at, with their angels and strange symbols. Nothing like the ones they use now days where the lawn mower drives right over the top of it. It is strange but when I'm in the cemetery, I feel at peace, not spooky like in the house. I'm not sure whether or not I want to come out here at night though, because sometimes late at night I see a strange glowing moving mists moving around out here. I wonder what it would be like to be out here on Halloween. When Jonathan walked through the cemetery with me, only a few of the names of his ancestors were familiar to Jonathan. He only recognized the most recent relatives. He didn't like being out there, said it gave him an awful headache and a bad feeling in his stomach, especially when he got close to his great-grandfather's tomb.

It was the largest and scariest in the cemetery. It stands 6 feet tall with a statue made to look like him, sitting on his stallion with a very large whip in his hand. He looks very angry. It was kind of creepy looking.

I think that the most fascinating part of the house is the attic where I spend many hours looking through the old trunks, boxes and crates. I imagine what it would have been like to live back in the early 1700 or 1800's, where women were so prim and proper, with their high neck collars and lace dresses and men were real gentlemen or they were supposed to be at least. That's the way I pictured it, like what you would see in *"Gone With the Wind."* I found pictures of people who I think might be Jonathan's family ancestors. There are several of the same men that look just like Jonathan. There is this huge old portrait over looking the main stairs of a mean looking man that looks like what Jonathan might have looked like maybe 100 years ago. I wonder if it is his great-grandfather, Nathaniel? Like most pictures, its eyes follow you everywhere in the room and you feel them on you even after you've left the room, really creepy. I sometimes hate walking up the stairs because I feel that he wants to jump right off the canvas and grab me. If you look at the picture long enough, you get the feeling that he could actually move right off that picture.

I have found some really cool old things in the attic, like tables, chairs, rugs, some lace curtains and doilies, crystal oil lamps and such and put them around the house trying to decorate it to look like it did so many years ago when Jonathan's great grandparents were alive. I could not believe it but I actually found a complete set of the finest china that I have ever seen in a box in the back of the attic. Of course, I took it down stairs and put it in the china cabinet for use when we have extra special guests.

Most of the furniture that his ancestors used is still in the house and still in very good condition, like the huge four poster bed in our room. I have noticed that some of the things I have put out have moved themselves to different spots. I put them back to where I want them, but they are moved the next day. Maybe someone or something in this house wants things his or her way, not mine. So after trying several times, I gave up and just left them wherever they end up. Telling the entities that the house really looks nice this way and since it was not good trying to fight the unknown I will let them have it their way.

Have you ever had that feeling that you're not alone when you are alone? That is how I feel in this old house, especially when I'm down in the basement. It was once used as some kind of root cellar or so I have been told. I have heard rumors that it was supposed to have been a slave hideout during the civil war, some sort of an underground railroad type thing. Jonathan has converted part of it to a sort of unfinished wine cellar.

Here, several miles out of town on this 200-acre plantation, I feel as though I am alone on a deserted island with no escape and nobody to talk to that understands how I feel about things. I wondered sometimes if I were to express my feelings out loud if someone or something, other than Jonathan, would answer me back.

I guess that I might as well try to comfort myself a little so I decide to take a long hot bath, maybe that will make the time go by faster and he will be home sooner. After opening a bottle of wine I pour myself a glass of wine, drink the whole thing at once and bringing the bottle with me I start going upstairs to the bathroom. I slowly climb up the velvet carpeted stair case being sure not to look at the portrait. I hadn't notice but it has started raining and wind is picking up. It is eerie hearing the wind hollowing through the trees and the eves of the house. It almost sounds like tiny screams. The sound of thunder comes from off in the distance. As a precaution I light some candles in the bathroom and my bedroom, I know how the lights will always go out when you're all alone, unsuspecting and unprepared. Pouring lavender and camomile oils in the bath water, I look out the window to see if maybe Jonathan is driving up the driveway. I see nothing but flashes of lighting off in the distance. As I count the seconds between the flash and the thunder, I know that the storm is still miles away.

The thought of Jonathan driving that long drive through these country roads when it is raining bothers me. So few people travel the road that if anybody had an accident it would be hours and hours before anybody found them. The closest town is several miles away and even in good weather over the bad road, it takes what seems, hours to get here.

All of the sudden, a flash from the lightening lights up the sky and the lights go out. Figures! When the thunder gets here it is so loud it is like having a freight train running through your house. The windows rattle, the fixtures on the walls rattle and shake. Boy, I'm surely glad that I lit some candles when I first came upstairs. There go those cold shivers again.

Slipping into the hot, steamy bubble bath, I feel warm all over or maybe it's just the wine. I finally start to relax and I drift off to sleep. I dream that I'm walking down a path. The path is dark, cold, mucky and wet, yet there is just enough light for me to see where I'm going. There is a musty, stale odor in the air. I hear the howl of a wolf and whirl around to see if it is here. I sense hungry eyes on me. I can almost feel its hot musty breath on me as I walk down the path. Each time I turn to see if it is there I see nothing except a dark shadow and a slight moving mist stalking me.

I come upon this steamy, bubbling, smelly, murky swamp. The path goes both to the right and the left around the edge of the swamp. Not knowing which way to go, I hesitantly take the left path, and it's covered with over grown vines and bushes. Trees have long twisted branches handing over the path, but it looks better than the other path which looked very, very muddy. The branches look almost like deformed, contorted arms with hands. I have not gone far before I come across a short man. He appears to be an ogre. He looks like the leprechaun from the horror movies you see around St. Patty's day. His head is all deformed but his eyes are very large and pierce right through me when he looked at me, sending shivers up and down my spine. He is sitting on a stump of an old rotten tree trunk smoking what looks to be some sort of pipe. The aroma from the smoke of his pipe is intoxicating, I feel dizzy as it circles around my head. He beckons me closer. I hear the cry of the wolf again which snaps me out of the trance. I feel it is above me, watching me but when I turn to look, it is not there, just the mist. The ogre says to me to watch out for myself for if I'm not careful I will become one of the lost soles in the forest. Before I could ask him what he means, he jumps off the trunk and scurries off into the dark swamp. Chuckling a wicked laugh.

There is a slight sound of rustling leaves, then the trees begin to move all around me, there is no wind. I watch mesmerized and fascinated that trees could actually move, without warning they grab me with a jerk. I feel the branches twisting around my ankles, moving up my legs, wrapping around my waist squeezing me. Quickly they move up my arms and onto my face. It feels almost as if they are touching me as a mother would be her newborn chid, at first gently caressing me, then as if they can sense my fear they start squeezing me harder, I feel my breath being squeezed out of me. I feel like I'm going to suffocate. "Help me" I tried to scream but it only came out as a whisper. I don't know why but the trees all of the sudden let me go and I'm falling. There is only this misty darkness all around me as I'm falling. All of the sudden this intense cold seizes me. When I finally hit ground, it is with a heavy thud. Laying there and gasping for air I wonder, what on earth is going on? My body feels broken, bruised, aching all over and I'm so weak I can hardly move. Slowly turning over, I look around for the trees or the ogre, but there is nothing there only darkness and silence. The silence so eery it makes my skin crawl. It's not my skin but the vines on the ground moving around me. Gasping for breath and aching all over, I force myself up trying to get away and find a way out of this retched forest before anything else happens to me. I don't see the ogre or hear the wolf but I feel that they are watching me from afar. Everything is so still, nothing moving. Why can't I see daylight? It's so dark. I try to run but there is something holding me back. Help me, I screamed in my brain.

I sense a presence all around me, but I see nothing. It feels evil! It moves in on me so quietly that it is upon me before I know it. Again I feel like I'm suffocating. The wolf is howling again, now in such a way it's like he was crying, crying like he has never cried before. The wind starts blowing softly at first then so hard that I can hardly stand. It's so cold. The presence is still there, I can't see anything, but I know something is all around me. I wish I could run, but I'm not able to move my arms or legs. The ogre was right I feel like I'm losing myself, to what I don't know, but I feel like I'm not anymore. I have no shape, no form, nothing. It feels like I'm floating mindless, bodiless, nothingness. Could this be what it feels like to be dead a voice in my head is saying to me? I shake my head to clear my thoughts.

The wolf cries again and again I'm falling, but this time when I land it's not solid, it's soft, mushy and smelly. My feet sink in and it's hard to move the ground feels like quicksand, now I'm afraid, so afraid I can hardly breathe. I feel terror, shear terror to a degree that no words can convey, I know that if I don't move, get out of here that presence will come and I will be no more. I'm struggling to get out, trying to get to solid ground, so I can run. The wolf cries again but this time it's an angry cry and its so close I can smell him. I start grabbing at things, trying to pull myself out of the mush. The presence is here. In the darkness I see something shaping itself out of thin air. It takes a shape, not human but a resemblance to a human form. It is a shadowy shape dressed in some sort of black cloak. It is standing on the ground in front of me and I feel terror again. I try to cry out but nothing comes, I have no voice. My voice has utterly failed me. Help me. I scream in my mind!

I cannot see the face, or its features, it has no life force, only a horrible smell of evil. I can't get away. Help me I scream but it is only in my head. It reaches out a hand its bony fingers pulling me toward it with its irresistible force. I have no power to fight him. I know that it wants to make me a part of this dark place. Its will has pulled me out of the swamp and onto solid ground without me knowing it. As I stand before it, I can feel the hairs of the wolf against my legs, his hot breath on my hands, but he is not there when I look down. Why am I here? Where is this place? What do you want of me? I have to get out. I have to find a way out, a ray of hope. Help me! The form has me before it, it says nothing but points to the ground, and forces me to kneel before it. It has the rotting stench of death all around it. I'm so afraid and recoil from the smell. I can't look upon it. This presence frightens me so. Won't somebody please help me?! The boney hand, reaches out and touches my face. As its hand touches my skin, I shiver from the horrible feeling of its cold rotting bones. I can't move. My breath is being drawn out of my body. It feels like it needs my life force to become human again, to do evil things, but why me?

The wolf is beside the form now, drooling and snarling. I can see his blazing red eyes staring at me. I'm so weak. I try to cry out but nothing comes out. I'm so afraid. I start to pray, not out loud, but to myself that this would soon be over. When the presence senses my prayers, it recoils its hand in disgust. Both it and the wolf cry out as if I had burned them or something. I know that they are trying to distract me but I continue to pray. I know how I can get out. I keep saying to myself, I do not fear, my soul does not fear, I know how I can beat this evil and this horrible place.

Chapter 2

The sudden ringing of the telephone snaps me out of my dream. Grabbing a towel, and trying not to slip on the wet floor, I dash to the bedroom to answer the phone. Before I can reach it, it stops, leaving an eery echoing ringing sound in the air. Even though I know that there is nobody there I reach for the phone anyway. As I put the receiver to my ear, "Hello?" I think I hear the sound of breathing on the other end of the line. I drop the phone stifling a scream. Now I'm really afraid. Shaking, I put the phone back on its cradle, praying that Jonathan would come home soon.

I have to control myself and my fears, it's only the storm. There really wasn't anybody on the other end. The lights will be back on soon. I have to look forward to tomorrow for it will bring sunshine, singing birds and Jonathan will be home.

So for now I'll just have to try to relax. I grab my book and climb onto our bed and snuggle down under the covers. Maybe that will take my mind off everything that has been happening.

Jonathan will be home soon, I hope, and all will be well. It seems like an eternity and a couple more glasses of wine, but I am so relaxed that I drift off to sleep again. Again, I find myself walking down a path. Only this time the path is different somehow and I feel as though I have some kind of a protective presence surrounding me. The path becomes brighter but this time it has taken me to the attic of our house. Here I have this strange feeling that I'm not alone. As I glance over the very large room, I see a misty figure of a woman dressed in a long white gown. There is a rich and delightful fragrance in the air. Who is she? She looks like some of the pictures I have seen in my explorations of the old trunks, but I can't quite make out who she is. She is pointing at one of the trunks. As I start to move toward the trunk but there is a clap of thunder and she disappears. Another figure appears but this time without facial features. I can tell that it is a man by the shape. He is holding a whip in his hand. I'm frightened of this figure and I can't seem to move, try as I may. The braided cord of the whip start crawling slowly across the floor toward me. I try to move my feet to get away from it, but I can't. It starts winding its way up my feet, ankles, upward around my knees. Then with a sudden jerk, I fall to the floor with a thud. The figure is pulling me toward it. I try grabbing at things to hold myself back but can't hold on. The figure starts laughing, a vicious, horrible evil laugh. I'd scream but nobody would hear me. Boxes start falling, hitting me as I'm being pulled across the floor. A doll falls out of one of the boxes, I grab it and throw at the figure. When the doll hits the figure, it screams. The thunder wakes me up.

I have this irresistible feeling that I have to go to the attic to see if what just happened really did happen. I have to find out who she was. What she wanted, and to try to find the trunk that she was pointing at. I have to try to find out who that male figure was, was he really there? I need to find that doll. Grabbing my bath robe, I ran to toward the attic stairs, but I trip over the carpeting and fall on the steps hurting my knees.

Limping now and going a bit slower, I climb the stairs leading to the attic. The creaky old steps echo throughout the house. The rusty hinges of the door squeal loudly out as I push the door open and reach inside for the light switch. But before I could turn on the light, I feel something grab my hand jerking me into the dark attic, I feel pain and all goes black.

I must have hit my head on something because when I come to, I can hear Jonathan calling for me from downstairs.

"Amy, Amy where are you?"

Pulling my aching and bruised body up, I limp down the attic stairs, calling out to Jonathan,

"I'm here, up the attic stairs."

He meets me half way up the stairs, gasping at the sight of me, rushes to me, taking me in his strong arms and carries me to our bedroom.

After letting him "doctor" take care of the bleeding bump on my head and my scrapped knees, I try to tell him what happened while he was gone, but he tells me to lie back and that I could tell him all about it in the morning. He goes to the bathroom and returns with a glass of water and gives me some sleeping pills and climbs into bed with me. As he is holding me, I feel safe and warm in his arms. It is strange laying in this huge bed knowing that someone in the family slept here before us, but now Jonathan is home and beside me I won't let that bother me. Trying not to think about it, the sleeping pills take over and I fall fast asleep, this time with no dreams, or at least none that I can remember. When I'm with Jonathan, it is as if he protecting me from having any dreams. But I have a feeling that maybe someone or something is watching over me, at least for now.

Morning brings bright sunshine and the sound of singing birds into our room. I wake up feeling sore all over, maybe it was from tripping on the stairs, maybe it was from my dream or maybe not. What it was that grabbed my hand in the attic last night? As I examine my wrist, there are no bruises, but it sure is sore to move. Before I could check my ankles Jonathan bursts into the room smiling and carrying a breakfast tray filled with all kinds of goodies and a beautiful red rose.

"Good morning, darling, I picked this rose fresh from our garden this morning just for you" he says as he bends down and kisses the top of my head. I start to apologize for the argument we had but he says,

"Let's forget it and pretend that it never happened."

Whole heartedly I agree. We share breakfast in bed and some much needed make up time. After a long hot steamy shower together, with more make up time, I'm feeling much better and looking forward to the beautiful day.

Jonathan suggests that since it's such a beautiful day we go explore the property to see what things we can find and maybe what mischief we can get into. We start out across the freshly plowed field of hay in the back of the house. It is so neat watching them as they bail the hay and stack them into stacks waiting for the trucks to come and haul them away. As we walk through the field we have to be careful because there are field mice and rabbits all around trying to get out of our way because now that the field is mowed they have no place to hide. There are even a few hawks swooping down trying to catch the mice as they race away, trying to find shelter.

Beyond the field is what Jonathan calls his "100 acre woods." When we get to the woods, it's like being in another place, it's so beautiful. The trees in the grove were so tall that from where I stood I couldn't see the tops of some. The trunks of the trees were huge, a lumberjacks dream. It reminded me of the Redwood Forest in Northern California. The scent of the trees, numerous plants and flowers were great, I had never smelt anything quite so wonderful before. There were so many different varieties of plants, trees and flowers that I would need an encyclopedia to even try to identify them.

Jonathan explained that these trees have been here since before his ancestors left the old country to come to America.

His great grandfather, Nathaniel, allowed part of the grove to be logged, at a good price to him, to make way for the hay field to be planted.

He showed me a path that he said would eventually lead us to a wonderful place. I asked him what the wonderful place was but he said I would have to wait and see for myself.

Being in these woods is so relaxing and peaceful, listening to all the birds singing and watching the little animals scampering about. The fresh air was intoxicating, the smells from the city are one thing I don't miss right now. It is seemed strange to find a path so far away from the house in the woods. Maybe all the other families that lived here before came out here and made this path maybe it goes to Jonathan's special place. So we slowly walk through the woods taking in all the wonders nature has to give. A short distance into the woods, we come across this babbling brook which is about 4 feet wide with a small waterfall. Jonathan tells me this is his special place. So we sit for a while soaking our feet in the cool water. While soaking our feet, I try to again tell Jonathan about my dream and what happened last night in the attic but again he says that he doesn't want to hear about it and since it such a beautiful day, let's not spoil it bringing up bad things. I wish that I had known about this place because I would have brought a picnic basket with us. This would be a great place to set up my isle and paint or just come out here when the things in the house start getting to me. We are going to have to come back here for a picnic.

After walking along the path for what seemed to be about a mile, we come across a large open meadow. Across the meadow was a stand of tall trees. As we got closer it looked very much like what I had walked in, in my dream. The meadow was full of all kinds of wild flowers. I made a mental note that I would pick some to take back to the house on our way back.

As we enter this stand of trees, the sun didn't seem so bright anymore, it was like a misty haze had just come over the area. I get this cold chill that ran up and down my spine and I shivered uncontrollably for a moment. The most strange part of this place is that there's no sound, the birds aren't singing, the crickets aren't chirping, you can't even hear the sound of the wind in the trees, no sound, nothing. If you stand still, it is as if you were in a sound proof room. It was so quiet that you could almost hear yourself breathing. It's an eerie and creepy place. I get this feeling that we are being watched but I can't see anybody. Jonathan doesn't seem to notice anything wrong and happily walks through the trees like he belonged among them. He said that he didn't know of this place because his Grandma would not let them cross the first stand of trees where the brook was to play when they were little. She said that beyond the hay field belonged to someone else.

At the very center of the stand was a great stone pillar circle with large stones that are about 6 foot high placed all around it. This place looks like what Stonehenge must have looked like hundreds of years ago. There is what looks like a huge flat stone pedestal in the middle of the circle. There is also a large fire pit close by. It actually looked as if somebody had used it very recently because it was full of ashes. There were dried flowers laying all around the stones. Jonathan said he was all of the sudden very sleepy. Laid down on the largest pedestal in the center of the circle and fell asleep right away. I tried to wake him but he wouldn't wake up. I felt very uneasy about being here but he wouldn't wake up. Since I couldn't wake him, I started looking around. As I walked around in this place, I guessed it must be a good 100 feet around the circle. There was nothing out of the ordinary placed around the perimeter of the circle just the stone in the middle.

There's that feeling of being watched again. I jerked around to look but there wasn't anybody there. I tried to pretend I was psychic and tried picking up the dried flowers so see if I could sense anything, nothing. Touching the stones, I got the shivers and this eerie feeling that something awful once happened here. I walked in and out of the stone circle wondering just exactly what would go on here. I let my imagination get the best of me and I started getting scared.

I hear what I think to be somebody calling my name. I without thinking called out, "Yes." I looked over at Jonathan thinking that maybe he was the one who had called my name, no, he was still sleeping. How could somebody call my name there wasn't anybody here but Jonathan and myself. Or were we alone? All of the sudden this feeling creeps back up and down my spine that we should get out of here and fast. This is not a place that I really wanted to be at right now so this time I shook Jonathan harder than before and made him wake up. Trying to hide my almost panicked state I say to Jonathan,

"I'm tired and cold, let's get back to the house before the sun goes down and we don't have enough light to get back."

Groggy and rubbing his eyes, he got up and we started back toward the house. I tried several times to get him to walk faster.

"There isn't any big hurry to get back to the house, enjoy the walk."

In my haste to get back to the house I forgot all about picking the flowers. After getting back into the plowed field my state of panic finally subsided.

Upon arriving back at the house there was a strange car in the driveway. It was this big old, shinny black car which looked somewhat like a hearse. The man in the car saw us coming, slowly opened the car door and gingerly stepped out. From this distance he looks as if he moved too fast he would break something. He was dressed all in black, right down to his shoes. When we got up closer to him his appearance changed and he looked younger, maybe it was the lighting, maybe not. He introduced himself as Dr. Frank Jefferson. He said that he had known Jonathan's grandmother for several years before she passed away. Said he wanted to come by and pay his respects to the family. Said that he has known the family for very many years, and felt that he was a historian on the subject.

Jonathan was very interested and, invited him up to the house for drinks. When I shook his hand, I got this cold shiver that I'll never forget. It was like touching a dead body. I felt that there was something wrong about him but I couldn't put my finger on it. It was as if I let him into the house something bad would happen. So, I suggested that since it was such a nice day we should sit on the front verandah and that way we could enjoy the late afternoon breeze, maybe even watch the sun go down. I said I would bring the drinks out and hurried into the house alone. From the look on the doctor's face he wasn't at all happy about not being invited into the house and having to sit outside on the verandah. He acted as if he was quite put out and gave me the impression that he wanted or needed desperately to go inside the house for some reason. I didn't care if he had to go to the bathroom or what, I was not going to invite him in.

Jonathan asked me to bring out some of the family albums so that he and the doctor could look at them. Maybe he could tell Jonathan who some of the people were. As the doctor talked, Jonathan jotted down notes of names and dates in the albums so we could look at them better later.

After a couple of hours listening to the doctor tell stories of the family, I grew tired and excused myself. When I got inside the house and looked up at the stairs I felt like something was beckoning me to come to the attic. I really didn't want to go up for it was getting late in the afternoon and the shadows in the attic play tricks on your eyes. After resisting the urge to go up, I finally gave in and went up there. I slowly entered the attic remembering what had happened before. Bringing a flashlight with me, I hurriedly turned on every light I could find in there so that I wouldn't be scared. This is one place I don't want to be after dark. It is nice during the day but spooky after dark! I was especially drawn to this old trunk, that I hadn't opened yet, as a matter of fact I hadn't seen it in here before. The lock on the trunk was covered with a hard waxy substance, much like they used to use to seal letters and such many, many years ago. It had a "C" stamped into it. It must be the family crest "C" stamp. I had seen it when they opened Jonathan's grandmother's will. Carefully pealing off the wax, I found that the trunk wasn't locked at all, so I opened the trunk. It was full of wonderful old clothes, it looked like hand made lace doilies, lace table cloths, lace curtains, beautiful hand made quilts, books, hat boxes, pictures, journals, even a couple of children's porcelain dolls, a child's sling shot and other things. I wondered if one of these dolls had been the doll from my dream the other night. Near the bottom of the trunk I came across a small jewelry box tucked inside some of the old clothes and was wrapped tightly with some very old lace. It was as if somebody was trying to hide it. I carefully removed the lace so that I might be able to use it later on something. Inside the box was a beautiful rose-colored cameo locket with an inscription on the back which read *"To Angela with love always and forever Morgan."* When I opened the locket, there was a picture of a man who looked just like the doctor sitting on our front verandah right now in it, but it couldn't be him because the date on the locket was dated 1812. I'm going to have to show this to Jonathan later when the doctor has gone home.

All of the sudden I got this feeling that I wasn't alone and was being watched. Jonathan and the doctor had come into the attic without making a sound and without me noticing them. When I turned around and saw them I jumped with a start.

"God, you two scared the hell out of me," I yelled at them.

They both laughed because of the look on my face and apologized for scaring me and for not saying anything when they came up.

"You looked as though you were a million miles away in thought and we didn't want to break your chain of thought," Jonathan said.

I don't know why but I hid the locket as though I was stealing something. The doctor noticed my uneasiness, tilted his head and raised an eyebrow but didn't say anything. For some strange reason when he looked at the contents of the trunk he acted as if he recognized the clothes inside and seemed to get this sad expression on his face. I thought I saw tears forming in his eyes. I'm glad that Jonathan is not observant and completely missed the look on the doctor's face. Now that Jonathan has "invited" the doctor into the house, I might as well face it doom is going to surely follow! Jonathan hadn't been in the attic before and was looking at all the great stuff.

"I'm going to have to come up here some time earlier in the day so that I can explore this place," he said gleefully.

Feeling very uneasy I said, "Well, it's getting dark, let's go down stairs and maybe if the doctor would like to stay for dinner I could fix us a light dinner."

"No, thank you Mrs. I can't stay." He politely said. Then added, "Maybe we can do it at a later date but for now I'll see myself out and let you two get back to enjoying your find."

After saying goodbye he left the attic. I told Jonathan I wanted to wait for a little while before going down the stairs.

"I have this feeling of distrust of our good doctor and I want to be sure he went right out and didn't linger inside the house to scare us later when we did come down stairs."

"Scaredy cat" Jonathan laughed tickling me.

Shortly thereafter we heard his car start up. I went to the attic window just in time to see his car drive down the driveway.

"Jonathan why did you let him in! I have a bad feeling about that. Kind of like he will bring bad luck or something terrible to our home now."

"Oh. There you go again, can't you just be happy that we have a friend here? Someone who knows more about the house and what happened here than anybody else and he can tell me about my family history. Things that I don't know and really want to find out." He said as he turned to leave the attic.

"Ok, but mark my words I don't feel good about it. Some people thought Dracula was a good friend too just before he drained them of all their blood after they "invited" him into their house." I said as I turned off the lights and followed Jonathan out of the attic.

After dinner Jonathan and I spent many delightful hours looking over the albums. Jonathan told me some of the stories the doctor told him. Some amazing, some not, like the ones about his great, grandfathers' cruelty to others. I asked him if the doctor remembered whether or not anybody had died here.

"Oh, don't start that again."

He stopped in mid sentence, with a strange look on his face said that the doctor had told him that some of his relatives did die here. His great-uncle, Zachary, hung himself in the basement, which in his time was a hideout for run away slaves. He continued on saying that his uncle had fallen in love with a young slave girl that worked in the house. He wanted to marry her and live as husband and wife here but Nathaniel wouldn't have anything to do with it. It wasn't allowed at that time in history and it was wrong for a white man to openly love or be associated with a Negro person other than as a slave, so Nathaniel had the girl sent away to prevent any embarrassment and/or shame on the family. They found out later that she was pregnant before they sent her away. Zachary knew that it had to be his child. He begged Nathaniel to tell him where he had sent her, so he could bring her back, but Nathaniel wouldn't tell him. Later by way of the underground railroad that Zachary and Jonathan's great-grandmother ran they found out she had been sent to some slave traders camp. When she refused the slave trader's attention, he had her shot claiming that she had been attempting to escape. Distraught over this, he hung himself. I wondered if Nathaniel hated slaves so much how and why did they help the run away slaves on his estate. Did he not know that they were doing it? I asked Jonathan if there were any stories about our room, the room over looking the cemetery or the attic. No, the doctor didn't say anything about them but would look through his boxes of family stuff to see if somebody might have written something in a ledger or something. I came across a picture that looked like the man at the top of our staircase. It was Jonathan's great-grandfather. Jonathan said his name was Nathaniel Alexander Chamberlain and that the doctor said he was a very cruel, hateful, viscous and controlling man and that everybody either feared or hated him. That if things weren't done exactly the way he wanted them, he would have anybody and everybody concerned whipped, tortured, shot or hung just to prove his point that he was lord and master. His great-grandmother Angela, had named the estate "Heavenly Acres," when they were first married but over time that name proved to be very wrong. After a while nobody, not even his great-grandmother, called it Heavenly Acres but called it by the nickname of *"Hell on earth."*

Slowly as the estate was handed down from generation to generation the memory of what had happened here died away along with the name. By the time Jonathan's grandmother got possession of the property there weren't many relatives alive to talk about the name or the bad things that happened here. All of the things that his great-grandfather used for torture and evil, the doctor told Jonathan was buried somewhere on the property and nobody knows exactly where. I came across a picture of a lady in a white lace gown that may have been the lady I saw or thought I saw that night in the attic. It was Jonathan's great grandmother's sister, Constance. Jonathan said that she had died sometime shortly after giving birth. Jonathan said that the doctor talked very fondly of her.

Just about then we heard the grandfather clock in the living room striking midnight, so we put things away and went upstairs to bed. Before retiring I decided to take a shower, while in the shower a shadow crossed in front of the curtain. Laughingly, I grabbed the curtain and jerked it open I said "Care to join me?" Jonathan wasn't in the room. There wasn't anybody in the room but me.

"Jonathan were you just in here" I called out.

"No, I just came upstairs, why?" He called from the bed-room.

Feeling like a fool I said "Nothing" and let it go at that. After getting out of the shower everything in the room was all steamed up but on the mirror were the words "Get out". I called to Jonathan to come look at the mirror but he was fast asleep. I wiped it away not knowing that to make of it. As I wiped it clean there was that woman's image again in the mirror stand-ing behind me. I wheeled around but there wasn't anybody there. Now I'm really not so sure I want to live in this house if these strange things are going to happen even when Jonathan is home. Snuggling next to Jonathan made me feel safer but not secure.

The next morning after a light breakfast we decided to drive into town to do some shopping. I asked about getting a dog but Jonathan still refuses to have one. He said that we don't need a dog and left it at that. I started to question his decision but thought I had bettered not spoil a very nice day. The drive, though long, was very nice. The sun was shining and there was a slight breeze. There were lots of trees, low rolling hills, meadows and lots of fields of corn, wheat and things, being not a country girl I couldn't tell what was in most of them. We seldom saw houses but when we did they were set far back from the road. It was strange, but we didn't see any people milling about on the places.

Our town isn't much to speak about. The typical small town with a General/Feed Store, a hair dresser, a rather nice looking café called the "Orange Blossom," the police station, the post office, a gas station/garage, an antique store, a few nondescript stores, a doctor's office. I wondered if Dr. Jefferson had an of-fice. He looked so old maybe he wasn't practicing any more. I couldn't tell because the sign out front just said medical/dental offices. I couldn't see any names from the street. Then there was the bank, it looked like it was built back in the 1800's, like something you would see Jesse James and his gang robbing in the movies. It was made of the old chimney block stone masonry that had that very well worn look. It looked to me like it would crumble in upon itself any minute. As we strolled along the streets, there weren't many people walking about but when we did meet anybody on the street they acted like we had the plague and avoided us. After shopping we decided to go to the café for lunch before heading back home. For being a small town the food at the café was wonderful, I was pleasantly surprised. Our waitress, said her name was Sally, and although quite polite didn't want to talk about much of anything other than to take our order, but at least she did smile when she saw her tip when we left. In the center of town is a large park with lots of trees and a rather large gazebo in the very middle and a lovely fountain quite close to it. The gazebo looked like the kind you would see in movies where the band would play and people would dance all night. The spray from the water felt good on my face as it had gotten quite hot outside, even though it was getting late in the afternoon. Watching the children playing in and around the pond made me feel better about the town. At least the children aren't stuffy. The people here were not overly friendly. I guess being new to town, you have to get used to being "a stranger." I hoped that would change after a while.

It was dark by the time we headed for home. We were almost home when we had to suddenly swerve to miss a person standing in the middle of the road. It was as if the person just came out of nowhere and stood there. Screeching our tires and sliding to a stop, we got out of the car to see if there was anybody there. Using flashlights we checked around but there wasn't any sign of anybody or thing on or near the road. It was if the person just vanished into thin air.

"I'll report this to the sheriff when we get home and have them check it out."

When we got home I was still shaken up from the incident on the road. I felt that there was something different about the house. As I walked through the back door in to the kitchen, I got this gut feeling that something bad was about to happen. Sure enough all of the sudden the walls and the floors seemed to be closing in on me, the windows and doors all slammed shut and there was this horrible ear piercing bellowing screeching sound coming from all around me. I screamed for Jonathan, who hadn't come inside yet, but he must not have heard me. I tried to rationalize this as just my imagination but it felt so real. As Jonathan walked up to the back porch and opened the door all went back to normal. I stood in the kitchen trying hard to catch my breath, my hands were shaking, my knees were weak and I felt like I was going to pass out.

"What's wrong. Are you sick? Do you want to sit down? Can I get you a glass of water or something?" He said as he grabbed me, helped me to a chair.

I asked him if he heard me screaming for him and he said that he hadn't. He didn't hear anything. I explained what had happened and he told me that it must have been my imagination because I was upset about that happened earlier on the road and that I'm talking crazy talk again or maybe I just had a panic attack. Whatever it is or was, it doesn't want Jonathan to know about it for now. Maybe it will show it's ugly head to him soon and he will believe me and that I'm not crazy. I took some sleeping pills in order to sleep, hoping all along that nothing else would happen tonight.

Chapter 3

Jonathan told me that he had to go out of town on a business trip and would be gone three or four days. I asked him if I could come along because I didn't want to stay here by myself. He said I couldn't come because he would be in meetings all the time, wouldn't be able to spend any time with me and that I would probably be bored. He tried to assure me that there was nothing here that would hurt me, it was just an old house, that old houses don't hurt people. People hurt themselves with their wild imaginations.

Laughingly he said "Why don't you invite the doctor over for tea or something."

"That's all I need. He would probably scare me so bad just be being here that I wouldn't sleep a wink while you are gone. No thank you. I will do just fine without him here" I said belligerently.

All went well for the first morning, but that early afternoon I thought heard the sound of weeping coming from upstairs.

Checking all of the rooms, I couldn't find anything. As a matter of fact, the weeping stopped when I opened the door to the guest bedroom that over looked the cemetery out back. Even though I knew that it was silly I called out "My name is Amy and I want to help you. Talk to me." No response, nothing but blessed silence. But I did smell the same perfume that I smelled that night in the attic.

Later in the day when I was in my bedroom I heard noises coming from the attic, like someone was moving things around in there. Then I thought heard music, and it sounded like a music box. Trying not to panic and determined not to let things get to me, I went down stairs and tried to ignore the noises by reading a book. I did my best to ignore it, thinking that it was just as Jonathan had said, my imagination playing tricks on me. I even went out to Jonathan's shop and looked around out there for a while. I even walked around in the cemetery taking pictures of different carvings on the headstones thinking maybe I'd paint something using the designs. I though that I had been outside long enough that whatever it was would get the hint and stop the music so I went back inside, it still had not stopped.

So, angry now, I went up the stairs to the to the first floor landing and called out "I'm not afraid of you. You're not going to get the best of me. You're not going to drive me out of this house. I promise you that!"

This extremely cold burst of air slammed into me almost knocking me down the stairs and I thought I heard someone say "You better be afraid." Ok, I tell myself this is an old house and strange things are going to happen. Determined to not let it get to me I thought that maybe if I actually go into the attic and say I'm not afraid that I'll feel better. The sun had been shining when I started up the stairs, but now as I got closer to the attic it seemed to be getting cold. I could see from the cut glass window that it was getting cloudy and grey outside. A howling wind had kicked up. I was shivering from the cold when I reached the door to the attic. My hand was trembling as I reached for the door handle, I could see my breath it was so cold. From the corner of my eye I saw a quick movement of a dark shadow behind me, I turned around to see what was there. I turned so quickly I tripped over this small wooden box that was laying on the floor next to the railing. I had to grab the rail to keep from losing my balance and falling down the stairs. That box wasn't there when I was up here before. The box had fallen open and several papers had fallen out. While I was picking up the papers, I didn't notice that the music box had stopped playing. Standing up and turning back to the attic door, I then noticed that the music had stopped. The sun was shining again, the wind had died down and it was warm in the house again, with that I decided to leave well enough alone. So I took the box of papers and went downstairs to see what I had found. The attic could wait.

"Whoever you are or whatever you are I have just about had my fill with you and your antics." I called to the attic as I walked away from the door, hurrying toward the stairs, pretending that I was not afraid but in reality I was scared and shaking in my boots.

Over a cup of steaming hot tea to warm myself up, I sat down at the kitchen table and opened my treasure. There were letters, maps, the candle used to seal the letters, receipts, the Chamberlain family crest stamper and all sorts of other things in the box. Curiously I opened and read some of the letters. There were several letters to Angela from family and friends. There were half-written letters from Angela to relatives. In a sealed envelope that was labeled Birth Certificates I found four birth certificates for her children and love letters to Angela from a Morgan stuffed inside them. She must have done this so that Nathaniel wouldn't find them. Morgan must have really loved her because in them he talked about taking her away from that mad man and starting their lives over somewhere else. These letters reminded me of the locket I had found and forgot to show Jonathan. I will have to do that as soon as he comes home.

As I examined the box more thoroughly, I noticed that there was a small concealed compartment in the bottom. I carefully pried the compartment open and found a diary, Angela's diary. It had that same sweet smell as that of the lady in the lady in the attic. This time I recognized the smell. It was Jasmine. I couldn't wait to read it. I wondered if it was her that was trying to tell me something because almost every time I smell Jasmine I find something. I wonder if this could be a clue as to what is going on in this house.

What a time for an interruption, the telephone rang and it was Dr. Jefferson. He was inquiring as to my health and whether or not Jonathan was home. I half lied and told him that Jonathan was out but I expected him home soon. Dr. Jefferson asked if he could have dinner with me because he had found something that he wanted to show me. Even though I still didn't trust him, I was curious as to that he had found so, I told him I would love to. I really needed some company because the noises in the attic were driving me crazy.

After about an hour, Dr. Jefferson showed up at my doorstep carrying a very large picnic basket. It smelled of fried chicken. I was surprised because I didn't know of anywhere in town to get that kind of a feast like that.

"Did you cook this?" I asked.

"No Mrs., my housekeeper fixed it after I asked if you would like to have dinner with me," he replied with his southern gentleman's manners just oozing at the seams.

Since it was still light outside, still not wanting him in the house, especially since I was alone, I suggested that we sit on the back porch over looking the field and woods and enjoy the afternoon breeze. This time he agreed with hesitation. As we ate, he told me that he had been searching his through some of his families' historical records and boxes and found a ledger that belonged to Jonathan's great-grandfather. He didn't know how the ledger came to be in his families things but he wanted Jonathan to have it. The ledger showed Nathaniel's financial dealings with merchants, banks and even the army, where he had bought and sold things to the union and confederate soldiers during the civil war. The ledger showed that he had made several large deposits in the bank after the war ended. It had the same name as the bank that is in our town. There was a Codicil to his will that was pushed into the back cover of the ledger addressed to the bank stating that when his great grandson *Jonathan Nathaniel Chamberlain* turned 30 and was living at Heavenly Acres, he was to inherit all the money in the bank. Dr. Jefferson stated that to his knowledge there weren't any children born into the family with the name of Jonathan other than my Jonathan. It was strange also because that was my Jonathan's exact name. This made us both wonder if the bank may be holding money in the bank for Jonathan. That couldn't be, because it was so very long ago and no bank would be holding a bank accounts that long, or could they? It was getting dark and the doctor excused himself saying that he would like to get home before it got too dark. He left the ledger with me.

I told him that I would show this to Jonathan as soon as he got home.

I wondered if this was confederate money, which as everybody knows isn't any good, but if it isn't, wow. I was so excited that I couldn't wait for Jonathan to get home so I called him. Unfortunately, he wasn't at his hotel when I called, so I left a message for him to call me as soon as he gets in, no matter how late. A puzzling thought came to me, HOW could Jonathan's great-grandfather be so sure that there wouldn't be any Jonathan's born into the family until my Jonathan? How could he be so sure that Jonathan's mother would name him Jonathan Nathaniel? How could he be so sure that Jonathan would live at Heavenly Acres and not his brother. Did Jonathan's grandma know about the account? How come nobody else knew of this account? Could this all be a hoax brought on by the good doctor? So many questions, I didn't have any answers for.

I got out the family albums and started looking for names,

in particular any pictures of children born into the family, to see what their names were. There were several places in the albums where pictures had been removed. Hopefully, Jonathan and the doctor, did that when they went through the albums. If they didn't, who did and why? I noticed that they did write some names down by the pictures. I found a few pictures of Constance, but no baby. I wondered what they did with her child after it was born. Was it a boy? Did it die before or after Constance and did they bury it in the cemetery out back along with Constance? I wondered if these questions could be answered by something from the attic, but it was getting late and I really didn't want to be up there after dark. The attic will be my priority for tomorrow whether Jonathan calls or not. I made myself a list of questions to ask Jonathan and if he couldn't answer them maybe the good doctor could.

Before going to bed I decided to read the diary. It began when Angela and Nathaniel first met and how happy they were. She told of how wonderful living in this house was going to be. She talked about when they were first married, what lovely stories she told. Then things started changing and she wrote of how Nathaniel started drinking, not heavy at first, but at time went on he drank more and more. He started having these severe mood swings and sometimes she would have to hide in her room to avoid seeing him. She stopped inviting lady friends over for tea because of his vulgar language. Things started getting really bad right after the birth of their first son, Christian. Nathaniel was jealous of the baby and wouldn't let her take care of him. He said that was what the nanny was for. Nathaniel was becoming overly aggressive with her and making her do things in the bedroom that she felt were not proper.

She wrote "Being a lady I cannot write, dear diary, what unspeakable things my husband has demanded of me but by God know that they are not proper. If I refuse him, I fear for my life."

When she would refuse him, he would go out to the slave

quarters. The next morning they would find one of the slave women severely beaten and hung from the large tree by the front entrance to the house so everybody could see her. He would tell Angela that it was her fault that happened. Nathaniel would tell her that if it were not for the slaves that would be her hanging there. Nobody would say that he did it but everybody knew he had done it.

After this incident she wrote "Dear Diary, Nathaniel is a beast and has murdered one of the slave women, oh how I wish I could free all of them and save their lives."

He was always angry, calling her names, saying that she was a pitiful woman. She tried not to get pregnant again but before Christian was a year and a half old she gave birth to the twin boys, Jacob and Joshua. Nathaniel told her that he never wanted those dam kids, that he wished they were all dead and Angela feared that he would kill them is she wasn't very careful. He made the nanny take complete care of the children almost never allowing her to be with her children. She was glad when he had to go on business trips. He made her go on some of the trips with him as a token wife. He always would embarrass her in front of his business associates. He even forced her to lie in their bed while he took a slave woman, which he made come with them on his business trips. Sometimes the nanny would sneak the children up the back stairs to her room so that she could see them at night before going to bed. He continued wanting her to do things in the bedroom against her will. There were several times he forced himself on her. She hated her sessions, as he called them, with him so she insisted that they take up separate bedrooms, of course he refused, saying you're my wife and you will stay in my bed at night. She would have to see the doctor after some of his sessions with her. The doctor advised her that she should would have to be more careful. She never told the doctor that it was Nathaniel's doing, only that she fell or something like that. Nathaniel never took his vows as seriously as she did. She had locks put on her bedroom door but Nathaniel would always find the key and force himself inside and force himself on her.

"Dear Diary, the doctor has told me that if I keep having these episodes that one day I might not come out alive. If only I could tell him that these "episodes" as he calls them are from beatings from Nathaniel."

Things changed a little after the birth of their daughter, Rebecca. Nathaniel actually became civil. He would lavish all kinds of things on Rebecca. When she was old enough, he took her traveling with him, leaving Angela and the boys at home. It was as if he only had one child and that was Rebecca. Angela would tell the boys that their father loved them also but that he didn't know how to show it and not to worry that he would never hurt them. The only times that she actually enjoyed living at Heavenly Acres was when Nathaniel was gone. After a while Angela refused to let him take Rebecca traveling with him fearing that he might start treating her as some kind of a sex object when she got old enough or worse. He went on a rampage, slamming doors, throwing things into the walls, cursing, telling her that she had bettered not sleep or he would kill her and take Rebecca away. So in order to get back at her he would lock all the children up in their rooms, not allowing food or drink for days telling Angela that this was all her fault and she knew exactly what he wanted from her if she wanted to see her children. Angela wrote "Dear Diary, I am forced to do the unspeakable things my husband wants of me for I fear for my children's safety."

Angela's trusted servants hated to see what was happening to the children and would sneak food up to them after Jonathan would drink himself into a stupor at night. For this Angela promised them their freedom and that when she left this hateful place they could come with her.

When Constance came to stay with them after the death of her husband, Nathaniel became even more hateful. Angela thought that Nathaniel was forcing his attentions on Constance because he wasn't abusing her so much anymore. There were several times when Constance would come down stairs in the mornings looks worse for wear.

"Dear diary, I fear that my husband had forced himself on my poor sister for today she came down to breakfast looking as if she had been beaten."

Angela tried to get Constance to put a lock on her door but she said that she was afraid to and wouldn't talk to her about what was happening to her.

There was his brother Zachary lived with them also he was supposed to be helping Nathaniel with the estate. Zachary, like Nathaniel, had a drinking problem to but, at least he would be go away for several days at a time. Nathaniel didn't want him be helping out with the handling any of the money for the estate, telling Zachary that their father left the estate to them both but that he had complete control of the estate because he was the older brother and there was nothing that Zachary could do about it. Zachary would abuse the woman in the slave quarters almost as much as Nathaniel. Nathaniel hated this and told Zachary several times that those slaves were "his" property and he had to leave them alone.

Angela wrote "Dear Diary, Zachary has become more like Nathaniel with each passing day. I feel that he too has been taking advantage of poor my poor sister. When I ask her, she wouldn't say anything just starts to cry, oh how I wish I could take all of us away from here so we could live happily again. But I fear that if I try Nathaniel will find us and kill all of us. I pray every night for a savior."

She even wrote several small notes about a Dr. M. Jefferson who would come to check on the children at first but then he would come on the pretense to see Constance.

"Dear Diary, could Dr. M be my savior? He is so kind and gentle. I feel like I could tell him everything and he would understand and take all of us away. But how would I tell him without Nathaniel noticing me? I have to find a way."

Angela had taken a liking to him and he to her right from the first time she laid eyes on him. She was afraid that if Nathaniel found out he would kill her and Dr. Jefferson.

"Dear Diary, Morgan has come again today my heart races so when I see him. I have to hide my face for I feel flushed and sure Nathaniel would see. I feel that if I look upon him and Nathaniel sees me do so it will be the end of my life."

One day after refusing Nathaniel he decided he would punish her by sending her children away to boarding school. After this she wrote "Dear Diary, Nathaniel has sent my children away to boarding school. I begged him not to but he would not listen. What will I do without my children, I feel that my heart will surely break, I don't know how I can go on? I must find a way to deal with Nathaniel for his rages are getting worse day by day."

Several of the pages had been torn out after this entry. I was getting tired, so I took the book with me to my bedroom. Laying it on the night stand I decided that I would finish reading it tomorrow. Unfortunately I didn't look closer at the back of the diary before I put it down or I would have noticed that there was a slit in the back binding.

Jonathan didn't call that night. He must have gotten in too late to call so I figured he would call me sometime during the day, so I took the extension phone to the attic with me so I wouldn't miss his call. After several hours of looking through boxes and boxes I didn't find anything that would lead me to any of the answers to the questions I had. I did find several pictures of family members in beautiful frames and decided that I would put them up in various place all over the house to give the house that lived in look. They would be great conversation pieces, now that we know some of the stories about them, when we had company come over. You know if this house has hidden passage ways and things, I wondered if there could be something hidden inside the walls up here. I started knocking on the walls to see if I could find any hollow spots. If a stranger had come in and saw me right about now they probably would have thought, I was crazy thumping on walls. I laughed at the thought. I gave up searching and went downstairs to the library where I thought I heard men's voices. Checking I found nothing but I did smell cigar smoke, so I left there and outside where I felt more comfortable.

Finally, Jonathan called and I was so excited I could hardly breathe. As I was telling him of the ledger, I talked so fast that he had to keep telling me to slow down because he couldn't understand me. Finally I after taking several deep breaths I calmed down enough to tell him what the contents of the Codicil said and about the money. He told me that his business would be wrapping up soon and he would be home as quickly as he could. In the meantime, he told me to inquire at the bank to see if there was an account. Before he hung up, he said "I thought you didn't like our good doctor." I ignored that.

The next day was bright, sunny and for being only eight in the morning it was getting quite warm. For being the middle of October it was rather quite warm. I thought it would have started cooling off by now. After a leisurely breakfast I drove into town thinking that the bank opened at 9:00 a.m. I found out that they really do, do things different here. I had to wait until 10:00 a.m. So walking down town I came across an antique store which was open and I knew I could spend at least an hour browsing. The store owner was wearing a pair of overalls that looked almost as old as he was. He was unshaven but his thinning grey hair was neatly combed back on his head. He was crewing on something, from the brownish stains on his fingers I figured it must be chewing tobacco. He eyed me curiously when I came in. Over the door was an old cow bell that clanged loudly when the door was opened.

"Hello, I'm Amy Chamberlain and I was wondering if you had any artifacts that might have come from the "Heavenly Acres" property or anything that might have belonged to the Chamberlain family."

He looked like he was going to say something but then stopped, spit and just said "Most of the stuff that might have come from the house, I'm told Dr. Jefferson would have." I asked him why would Dr. Jefferson have them.

"I'm told there ain't any living relatives that's why" he said with a snap.

I explained to him that Jonathan and his brother, Samuel, were in fact living relatives of Amelia and Craig Chamberlain, who were their grandparents. He said that he didn't know that she had any grandkids. That puzzled me because they had lived all of their lives here and most everybody knew either them or one of their family. Didn't they tell anybody that they had grandsons, didn't they ever come into town? The store owner said that Mrs. Chamberlain didn't come into town much especially after her husband died and her son and daughter-in-law were killed in that car crash. He knew about Jonathan's mother and father but not of Jonathan and his brother, why? He said that the best place to get any answers would be Dr. Jefferson. I gave up because he wasn't going to say anything even if he did have any artifacts, so I set my mind on shopping. I did find some really old nice things that I thought would look nice in the house, spying others that I would come back to get at a later date, but for now the bank was my concern.

Finally after purchasing my things and putting them in the car, it was time to go over to the bank to check on the account. Maybe they won't talk to me either. Maybe they too don't know that Amelia had grandsons like the store owner.

There was only one other customer in the bank when I came and he quickly left, I guess he thought I might be bank robber or something. I asked for the bank manager and the teller raised her eyebrows. I assured her that I was not a bank robber that I just needed some information.

"Maybe I can help you," she politely said.

After I explained why I was there she went straight to the bank manager's office and out came the manager. Mr. Collins was a pleasant but rather over weight man wearing a rather odd colored striped suit which smelled of cigar smoke and sausage.

"Hello, my name is Amy Chamberlain, wife of Jonathan Nathaniel Chamberlain the new owners of Heavenly Acres, and I'm here in regard to this".

I handed him the ledger, the Codicil and the Nathaniel's Will. After looking over the documents and looking quite pale, he politely told me that he could not help me that Jonathan would have to come in himself and then excused himself rather quite rudely, wiping perspiration from his brow, walked away rather quite quickly, went straight into his office, closing the door behind him. So, there I was holding all these documents and feeling like I was totally unwanted in their bank and angry for being treated so rudely. That feeling of total mistrust and being unwanted was really something I didn't like about the town. Before I left the bank I could see Mr. Collins peaking out his Venetian blinds to see if I had left yet.

Chapter 4

So with hurt feelings I drove back home, stopping to buy some fruit and vegetables from a fruit stand on the way. It was mid afternoon when I got home, after putting the groceries away and being pleasantly surprised nothing happened, I called Jonathan explaining to him what went on. He said that it was ok and he would take care of it. I asked when he was coming home.

"I'll be home before you can say Rumpelstiltskin."

With that I heard someone giggling, turning around there he stood in the dining room holding a bouquet of roses. Boy was I glad he was home I ran to him throwing my arms around him and smothering him with kisses, promising that there would be much more of that to come later.

After showing him the finds, I got from the antique store I explained to him that the store owner didn't know that he and his brother existed.

"The man who owns the store wasn't there when we were growing up so naturally he wouldn't know of us."

"Why would Dr. Jefferson have things that belong in this house when your grandmother just recently died?" I asked.

"Maybe, he was asked to be the caretaker of the house after grandma died, I don't know. You know the house was vacant for a while before we came here. We'll call Dr. Jefferson tomorrow and see what he has to say on the subject, ok? But for now let's get reacquainted."

With that he took me in his strong arms and carried me up the stairs to our room. When we got there, there were candles lit, a bottle of champagne on ice and chocolate-covered strawberries waiting for us.

"You sneak, how long have you been waiting for me to come home? I didn't see your care when I drove up."

"Not too long, just long enough to get this set up to surprise you and I parked around back just so I could surprise you."

"I love you" I cooed.

He laid me gently down on our big bed and started kissing me from head to toe paying attention to all the good spots in between.

I don't know why but I had one of my strange dreams again this night. The strange thing about the dream was that I wasn't in a swamp. This time I was outside our house in the cemetery. A great fog covered the ground when a white glowing shape appeared before me. I could just barely make out the clothing it was wearing. It looked to be uniform of a civil war soldier but I couldn't make out a face. I heard a voice saying "beware" then it was gone. Next I was standing before the door to what looked like Jonathan's workshop. The door creaked ever so slowly open but when I went inside it wasn't his workshop at all. Inside it was the old barn as it was in Nathaniel's time. There were slaves moving about cleaning the barn, the horse stalls, a tackle room and what looked to be grooms quarters. This very loud angry voice came from behind me, I turned and there was

Nathaniel Chamberlain sitting on his stallion as if he was a king or something. I thought he was going to run me down but he didn't move. He had the most evil and angry look on his face that I had ever seen. He started yelling at the slaves hitting and whoever came near with his whip, telling them that they were lazy, good for nothings and that this barn wasn't fit enough even for them to live in. One unfortunate slave fell to the ground and Nathaniel's face took on the look of great rage. Laughing he urged his stallion toward the man on the ground. Angry because the horse didn't want to move at first, he started beating the horse with his whip and kicking it as hard as he could.

"Move you foul beast. Move dam you!" he yelled.

He caused the horse to trample all over the slave, crushing his skull. The sound of the crushing bones were sickening.

"Let that be a lesson to the rest of you! Now get this barn cleaned up and get rid of that", he said pointing to the lifeless body laying in a bloody mess.

There was a bright flash of light, when I was able to see again, I was in the basement of our house. It too was as it was in Nathaniel's time. I saw a man who looked like the pictures of Zachary standing near a wooden box. He was sobbing, sobbing so hard that his whole body shock. One end of rope was tied around his neck, and the rope was tied to the rafters. He slowly got up, and stepped on the box. The way he stepped on the box it teetered in a manner that if he moved just right it would topple over.

"Oh Topieta my love, why did they send you away? I can't go on without you, I won't go on, maybe we will be together someday, somewhere. May God forgive me for what I'm about to do?"

With that he stepped off the box that held him up. Just then Angela was coming down the stairs, hearing the cracking of the beams she hurried down the stairs. She screamed when she saw his body hanging from the rope. His face turning blue, eyes bulging out, gasping for air and twitching as the last bit of life drained from his body. There was another bright flash of light.

Now I'm in the woods, at the stone circle. There are several hooded figures swaying to and fro in the middle of the circle. A great fire was burning in the fire pit. They were chanting something but I couldn't make it out. They were beating the drums wildly. There was a strange smell in the air. It was intoxicating. I could feel my body swaying to and fro like the hooded figures. There was one person who wasn't hooded. He was completely naked except he had on what looked like some kind of head-dress. He was dancing and jumping around the fire. All of the sudden he appeared right in front of my face startling me.

Again the bright light, only this time I'm back in my own bed. Jonathan was opening the curtains in our room letting in the sun light.

"Wake up sleepy head, time for another great day. Breakfast is ready and waiting in the sun room", he grabbed my robe, handing it to me. As he helped me into it, I said,

"Jonathan, I had this really strange dream last night."

"Tell me all about it downstairs over breakfast, darling. I'm starving."

I told him about my dream over breakfast and asked him what he thought about it.

"Great imagination, what did you eat or drink before you went to bed last night? Oh yeah, this old house is playing tricks you again right?"

I wish just once that he would take me seriously. Someone or something is trying to tell me something and Jonathan just won't listen.

We arrived at the bank, all documents necessary in hand. Mr. Collins greeted us with a bright and cheery smile. "May I help you?" he asked. "I'm Jonathan Chamberlain and I'm here to inquire about the account my great-grandfather Nathaniel Alexander Chamberlain left to me. Here is his Will, the Codicil to the Will, the ledger regarding the money, a letter from

Dr. Frank Jefferson identifying me, my drivers license, social security card and my birth certificate. That should be enough information to check on the account."

"Well now let's just sit down and see what we can come up with, shall we."

It didn't take much looking for the look on his face and the fact that most of the color drained out proved that he found something. I thought he was going to faint.

"Are you all right?"

"I need a glass of water" he said very weakly, "Ceyla bring me a glass of water" he said just barely over a whisper.

After a few moments he composed himself he looked at Jonathan, bent over as if someone would hear him speaking and said in a whisper.

"There is more than six million dollars in this account."

"You're kidding, right" Jonathan said jokingly.

"No, here see for yourself. Looks like there have been numerous deposits throughout the years and the whole account was updated by your grandmother a couple of years ago with your name and social security number on it."

We all sat there in silence, dumbfounded and in disbelief for a while.

"Please be assured that I don't have any intention of taking the money out of your bank at this point in time. Well, I guess I won't have to worry about much from now on, right? But I am going to make arrangements to give one-half of it to my brother at a later date."

After making a small withdrawal and fixing the account so that it was in both our names, we left not really knowing what to do next. So we drove for a while until we came across a great looking Bed and Breakfast which was set on the edge of a beautiful lake and checked in. As we relaxed in the late afternoon sun on the veranda, sipping Pina Colada's, we talked about the things that we could do and places we could go with that money.

After arriving home three days later Jonathan set out first to write to his brother Sam, who is on location as a big game photographer for some animal rights magazine and let him know what happened at the bank and asked him to let him know a bank account where he could transfer some of the money to him.

It was a warm day out so Jonathan suggested that we should spend the day exploring the basement, since it was cooler there and we could look in the old boxes and things to see if there were going to be any more surprises in store for us. After spending what seemed to be hours of looking in old boxes, we came up with lots of things we could use upstairs to decorate the house but nothing "juicy" about the family or any hidden surprises.

One surprise we did find was hidden behind some of the old boxes that were stacked along one wall. We found this old boarded up door in the wall, the hinges and the door handle was rusted over. Jonathan found a crowbar and pried the door open. As the rusted old door creaked open, a stale musty cold breeze billowed out from the dark beyond. Jonathan took a flashlight and shined it down into the darkness. We could see that it was a long, long tunnel of some sort. The dirt floor looked like it hadn't been walked on in many years. We ventured into the tunnel, we found old oil lamps oil still in them, hung from on hooks in the ceiling. We lit each lamp as we went down through the tunnel. An eerie feeling came over me that this was not such a good idea and asked Jonathan if we could just go back to the basement and forget doing this right now.

"Chicken, Amy's a chicken, bock, bock" he chimed as he walked on acting like a chicken. The tunnel had several side chambers that led off in each direction. As we checked each side chamber room, we found that some of them looked as if somebody had once lived there. Could this have been make shift homes for run away slaves? I wondered if this was the old underground railway tunnel they used when they smuggled the run away slaves out. There was some dust covered old boots, blankets, a few bunks with bedding on them, on one of the beds I found an old doll that probably once belonged to one of the run away slave children, cloth bags that looked like very old suit cases, clothes, dishes and all sorts of other things lying all around on the ground. It even looked as if they had a fire pit, for cooking in some of the out tunnels because we did find some old pots and pans. Some looked as if they still have food in them but by now they were petrified. After walking for some time we came to a dead end, or so we thought it was. As we looked around my flashlight hit upon a dirt and vine-covered ladder that looked like it hadn't been used in many years. It lead to a door in the ceiling of the tunnel. The old ladder creaked terribly as Jonathan stepped on it. As he was getting close to the top of the ladder, one of the rungs broke and he almost fell. I screamed, but since the tunnel was made of dirt the sound was muffled and didn't go anywhere. Jonathan said he was all right and kept on going. When he got to the top, he pushed on the door, dirt and hay fell down in a large cloud covering him so that I couldn't see him for a while, all I could hear was him cursing and coughing. When the dust settled, he looked almost ghost like covered in all that dirt. I started laughing and said that he looked like one of his relatives come back from the grave.

"That's not funny, now hand me the crow bar so I can get this thing all the way open, thank you very much," he said with a huff.

Finally, he got the door lose enough to push it all the way open. Some of the old boards broke as he pushed on it. He slowly moved the rest of the way to the top of the ladder, poking his head through the opening and shining his flashlight into the darkness above.

"It's an old room in the barn" he said with amassment, "Come on up but watch that step," he called when he got up in the barn.

As I carefully climbed the ladder, I could imagine how the

slave felt doing exactly what I'm doing now. Afer getting up inside the room, I knew that this was where Jonathan's great-grandfather had beaten his slaves because this place was exactly the way it was in my dream. But this part of the barn was boarded up into a smaller area. I know that the barn was much, much bigger, or at least it looked like it was from the outside. Using our flashlights, we could see that on one of the walls there were some boxes stacked on shelves. When we opened the boxes, we found that they contained very old pictures. Some of them looked like ones we have in the family albums in the house. But there were some that showed people being tortured, some of dead people and there was even some that looked like our good doctor, Jefferson doing horrible things to people. One showed the doctor standing very close to Angela, almost too close. Constance was in the background with a very hurt look on her face. I wondered if Angela was having an affair with the doctor and he was really supposed to be Constance's beau.

Let's take these pictures and things back to the house so that we can look at them further," I said sort of asking, wanting to get out of there.

"That's a good idea" Jonathan replied. " I don't want to go back the way we came."

"Look here there's a box of old books, maybe they have some-thing in them about your family. I'm going to take them back to the house also."

Jonathan started feeling the walls for a door, a door handle or something that would let us get out of here. In one corner he tripped over something on the floor. It was a large dirt mound in the floor. Jonathan ignored it at first but then when he flashed his flashlight on it, it looked like an old rug covering up something. The boards in the walls of this part of the barn were so close together that hardly no light could get through and it was really dark in here. The flashlights that we brought didn't seem to shed enough light so we looked around for an old lamp or candle or something that would give more light. Nothing could be found.

"Jonathan, can we break out one or two of the boards from the wall to let in some light?"

"Yeah, or you could go back down in the tunnel and bring up an oil lamp," Jonathan said.

"No that's ok, lets just break the boards, ok" I replied.

Thankfully, Jonathan had brought the crow bar up with him. So after a bit of prying with the crow bar, he finally got a couple of boards off, then another and another. What a joy it was to see the light of day and to get some fresh air.

"What do you want to do about the oil lamps we lit in the tunnel?" I asked.

"Forget about them, they didn't have much oil in them anyway and they'll burn themselves out, unless you want to go all the way back and blow them out one by one" he said with a laugh.

"No way I'm not going down there again by myself" I exclaimed.

Jonathan turned his interest back to the rug. Using the crow bar, it took a while for him to dig up a small box hidden underneath the rug. When he finally got it up, it looked to me more like a tiny coffin than a plain, wooden box. This cold shiver came over me as I touched the box jerking my hand back and rubbing it like I had just been burned.

"Let's not open it here, I'm afraid of what we might find in it" I begged.

"Let's take it outside, ok?"

"Ok."

We had to break a few more boards out of the wall to get the box out. When we finally got out the heat of the day made me realize how good the sun felt. How horrible it must have been for the slaves to be cooped up down in those tunnels not being able to see day light for days maybe even weeks at a time. I prayed that having to stay down there was worth it for them.

We took the box around to Jonathan's work shop to open it. Setting it down on the bench, Jonathan pried the lid off.

Both of us stood there not knowing what to say or do next when we saw the contents of the box.

In the box was the skeletal remains of a small child wrapped in very old lace, with a red satin cloth covering it's face. Could this be the baby that Constance lost? Was this one of the slave's children?

"Should I call the sheriff and turn this over to him to check out?" I asked.

"No, let's call Dr. Jefferson first, maybe he can shed some light on this."

Dr. Jefferson showed up about an hour later.

"What is it that is so important that you couldn't tell me about it over the phone Jonathan?"

"You'll have to see for yourself" Jonathan said as he led the doctor out to the workshop. I thought that the doctor was going to faint when he saw what was in the box because all the blood drained out of his face.

"Oh, my God" was all he could say over and over. Reaching for a chair, the doctor sat down for a while. After a while the doctor asked if we could bring the box back up to the house because he could use a good stiff drink. That was ok with me but I made them leave it on the front verandah because I didn't want it inside my house.

When the doctor finally composed himself enough to look in the box again.

"If I'm correct, and I pray I'm not. These remains may belong to one of your family members. I will have to do some tests to be sure."

"How are you going to be able to tell who it was?" Jonathan asked.

"I will need to take some of your blood for the DNA tests. Maybe we'll be able to find out who this poor child might belong to."

"Do you think that there might be more remains buried in that old barn?" I asked.

The doctor thought about it then said "Don't go snooping around in the barn too much because if there are more remains out there the sheriff might want to look at them first."

"If there are more remains, what if anything, could the sheriff do?" I asked.

" I don't know but I'm sure that he would be interested, so don't do anything until you hear back from me. Ok? Oh, by the way did you find anything else while you were out there?" he inquired.

"We found this old tunnel that led from our basement to the old barn, but it looked like it hadn't been used in a hundred years. Why do you ask?"

"Just curious, that's all. That old tunnel was where your great-grandmother and your great-uncle Zachary hid run away slaves and helped them escape. Nathaniel didn't know about it. If he did, he would have killed all that was involved. There are several side tunnels where some of the families stayed for periods of time while waiting for the right time to escape. You might find some very interesting things down there if you want to explore it."

"No, thank you. It creeps me out" I replied looking at Jonathan who was about to say something.

"I'll go for now and I'll be back in touch with you in a few days."

After saying our good byes the doctor and the box disappeared from sight. Which made me feel better seeing the box leaving. I really hope there aren't any more surprises waiting for us in that part of the barn. I know there wasn't anything under the part of the barn that we renovated because we put in plumbing and new flooring. I wonder why we didn't notice the part of the barn that was boarded up.

It was several weeks before the doctor got back to us, letting us know that the were not the remains of a family member and that it was those of an African American child. I wondered if it was the slave Nathaniel killed in my dream or was it a dream? We invited him over for drinks and to tell us all about the story he promised to tell.

He started by telling us that even though these remains was a family member he really wasn't sure who they were. He explained that Constance had a baby that had died and it could possible be that child. His family told him that Nathaniel told her that the child was a bastard child because she wasn't married and it could not and would not be brought up here and that she would have to leave. Angela begged Nathaniel to let her stay at least until after the child was born and that Constance would leave when they were both able to travel. Nathaniel didn't want Constance to stay either so after she had the baby he took the infant away from the midwife and they never saw it again. Even though Angela constantly begged him to tell her what he had done with the child, he wouldn't. He told Constance that her baby died after she gave birth and it was buried in the cemetery. For several months Constance would sit in the cemetery at what she was told was the grave of her baby. Then one day they found her dead in her room. The story has it that she died of a broken heart.

"Who was the father of the child?" I asked.

"Well, I have to tell you that Morgan Alexis Jefferson who was my great-grandfather wrote in his journal that she and him were married. He believe that by doing this it would allow him to see Angela without any suspicion from Nathaniel."

"Wait a minute, I found a locket in the attic that belonged to Angela that was inscribed "To Angela with love always and forever Morgan." I blurted out before I could stop myself because I hadn't told anybody about the locket until now. Jonathan looked at me with a surprised look on his face.

"Why didn't you say something about that before now."

"Well, so much has happened since I found it, it just slipped my mind" I said kind of embarrassed.

"I'll get it so that you can see it and I also found Angela's diary that might shed some light on this also I hope " I called as I was leaving the room to retrieve the locket. I returned with the locket and Angela's diary to show them what she had written about Dr. M. J.

"Here, see the inscription."

"Here is what Angela wrote in her diary about him also. Angela also wrote that she thought that Nathaniel and Zachary were taking advantage of Constance, so maybe one of them was the father. Wait a minute. I saw a picture of Morgan, Angela and Constance in the album. Here, see. It looks almost like he was secretly holding hands with Angela as Constance looked on."

"That cad," the doctor declared.

"Doctor, Morgan looks very much like you."

The doctor picked up his drink and took a long swallow.

"Yes, I know. He caused my family and yours much grief. He was in fact very much in love with Angela and yes it is true that he married Constance just so that he could be near Angela. You see Nathaniel was a very jealous man and suspected that there was something going on between Morgan and Angela. Constance was truly in love with Morgan and thought that if she had a child that would make him want her. But alas she was dead wrong. He wrote in his journal that after he found out she was with child he knew he couldn't be the father for she was to far along. He didn't care that the child on the way he was going to find a way to take Angela away from here and start a life somewhere else with her not Constance. He was very happy after he was told that the child had died, but if he had known that Nathaniel had taken it, there probably would have been all out war. Constance did not just die of a broken heart, but Morgan helped her. She told him that she was going to tell Nathaniel everything about him and Angela if he didn't go away with her. Angry over this he started slipping of some kind of poison in her food and drinks. Knowing that when she died it would look like a natural death. He thought that with her out of the way, he and Angela could get away sooner. But one of the maid servants who loved Constance saw what was happening and informed Angela. Angela loved her sister very much and after finding out what he was doing, she refused to leave with him. Unfortunately it was too late to save her sister because she died a couple of days after Angela found out what was going on. Angela told Morgan she would rather die at the hands of her hated husband than live with him knowing what he had done. She even threatened to tell Nathaniel of what he had done if he didn't go away and leave her alone. He was a broken man and cursed Nathaniel and everyone that came after him. Half crazed he planned to get rid of Nathaniel and force Angela to go away with him anyway. His journal ended there."

I asked several of my family members that are still alive if they could tell me what happened after that but all they would say was that he left the area. Nobody wants to talk about him. Jonathan who had been listening very intently looked as if he couldn't believe the story the doctor had just told.

"No way did any of that happen. You're making that up. I'd have to see that journal to believe any of this," he said as he shoved the diary, the locket and several pictures off the table before he stormed out of the room and out of the house.

The doctor and I looked at each other in disbelief of his outburst. As I picked up the diary the back binding came off and a letter fell out. It was addressed to Morgan from Angela.

It read, "My dearest darling Morgan, please know that I have loved you from the moment I first saw you. I know what you did to Constance was because of your love for me. I forgive you. I cannot think of living without you my dearest. Forever yours, Angela"

"If only Morgan has seen this letter. I wonder why it was tucked inside her diary? Why didn't she get it to him somehow?"

"Maybe Nathaniel interrupted her before she could deliver it or have it delivered to Morgan." I said.

"It sure would be interesting to find out what happened to Morgan after that. Do you know if he left this area or stayed on over at your place and never to see Angela again?" my curiosity was getting the better of me.

"I have to look more through the old boxes to see if there is anything that tells what happened to him and I'll get back to you on that, I'm interested in knowing also. Well you had bettered be looking for your husband. He didn't look too good when he stormed out of here. I'll let myself out, call me when you find him."

For the first time since I met Dr. Jefferson I felt as if I could almost, almost trust him.

I looked for the better part of an hour before I finally found Jonathan sitting on the great pedal in the stone circle.

"Jonathan, what is wrong with you? That was not very nice the way you stormed out. The doctor looked as if he had really hurt your feelings or something and I might add he was hurt also." I asked angrily.

Jonathan looked up at me as if I wasn't his wife and said with a very distinct growl, "Get out of here and I don't want to talk about this not now!"

That really took me by surprise for I had never seen Jonathan get mad like that. Being just a little afraid I decided that maybe it was best that I did leave him alone for now, so I slowly walked back to the house thinking that he would catch up and apologize for his rudeness, but he didn't. I fixed his favorite dinner. Set the dinning table just right, thinking that, that would help but he didn't show up for dinner either. As it was getting dark outside and I started looking every few minutes out the window hoping to see him. Finally I turned on the big outside light to show him the way back to the house. Just as the grandfather clock was striking midnight he came in the door. I told him hat there was dinner waiting for him in the oven if he was hungry. He didn't say anything just went up the stairs to our room. After he went up stairs, I called Dr. Jefferson to let him know that Jonathan was home. He told me that if I needed anything to call him. I thanked him and hung up. Staring at the stairs I was kind of scared to follow him up there so I waited a few minutes before going up. I knocked gently on the door to let him know that I was coming in and found him laying on the bed staring up at the ceiling.

"Jonathan," I said almost in a whisper.

He didn't answer. I moved closer to the bed, "Jonathan" I said again a little louder this time.

"I'm not Jonathan women and you know that" came a booming voice as he turned his head slowly toward me I was so startled it caused me to stagger backwards. Cold shivers ran up and down my spine.

"What do you mean you're not Jonathan?" I asked.

"Get out of here before I strike you down women" came the voice again louder this time as he sat up on the edge of the bed. This scared me so that I quickly left the room, without me touching the door, the door slammed behind me as I went into the hall. I stood there not knowing what to do, thinking that there has to be a reason for all of this, but what? All of the sudden it hit me like a lightening bolt, could Nathaniel's spirit have taken over Jonathan's body after hearing what the doctor told us about Angela and Morgan? That's impossible, things like that just don't happen, or do they? Here goes my imagination again.

I sat outside the door on the floor for quite a while until I started getting cold. When I got up, I found myself walking toward the attic. Maybe I'll find something in the attic to help me with this problem. After spending a while looking for something, anything, I gave up. I tried to call the lady I had seen before but nothing. I called upon Angela still nothing. Maybe I just thought I heard Jonathan's voice change and what he said could have been my imagination, right? Tired and confused I started back to our room to check on Jonathan again. Upon reaching our room I heard the shower running, he was singing to himself.

"Jonathan are you all right?" I quietly asked.

"Yeah, I'm fine. Why do you ask?" he said puzzled.

"I thought that what the doctor said disturbed you," using the word disturbed very carefully.

"I don't know what you are talking about, I'm hungry where's dinner."

Now I'm really confused but he seems to be all right, for now. I was afraid to say anything about what had transpired that afternoon so I let it go for now.

Chapter 5

Jonathan had to go into town today and against my better judgment, I called Dr. Jefferson and told him what had happened and was hoping that maybe he would have any suggestion as to what was going on. He said that, that was not his expertise so he would have to talk to a colleague of his to see if may he could help. He said it would take a couple of days but he would call me to let me know if he found out anything. I told him that he would have to do it without Jonathan knowing about it because he didn't remember what had happened. He assured me that Jonathan wouldn't find out.

When the doctor finally called, he said that his colleague wants to come to the house to talk to Jonathan and to check out the house. I told him that, that was out of the question because Jonathan would never allow it. The doctor suggested that maybe "they" could stop by on a social visit and then he could on the sly question Jonathan. I knew that Jonathan sometimes doesn't catch onto what is going on so I thought that maybe a social call wouldn't hurt. So I told the doctor that when Jonathan comes back from his business trip we could have a brunch or something like that so it wouldn't look like his friend was there on a "medical" call so to speak.

Strange things started happening after that. When I was by myself upstairs one day, I heard heavy foot steps stop outside the bedroom door and then walk away. I even saw a shadow on the floor going by the bedroom when the door was closed and I was inside. Once the door knob started moving by itself. I quickly opened the door to surprise who or whatever it was outside the door but there was anything there. Jonathan's clothes were taken of the hooks in the closet and crumpled on the floor. When I would tell Jonathan about these things none of this seemed to bother him, telling me that I must have done it and didn't remember. There were words written in my lipstick on my vanity mirror that said "Get out." When I told Jonathan about this, he seemed a little concerned, but when he came to look at it, the words were gone. He thinks I'm going crazy. One night the telephone rang, I insisted that Jonathan answer it because when I would there would be no one there only breathing. He did answer it but it was just a dial tone when he said hello. He looked at me, shrugged and said "Wrong number."

In a few days' Jonathan had to go out of town again. This time he said that he had to be gone a month in order to close this real estate deal he was working on.

"Why don't you have one of your friends from the city come and stay with you while I'm gone."

"That's a great idea. I'll call Natasha. She has nothing to tie her down to staying in the city and probably would love to come to the country and help me explore this old place. We could go into town, shop at your favorite antique shop or just hang out around here" I said excitedly.

When I called Natasha to ask her to come, I thought she was going to jump through the phone she was so excited. She showed up on our door step in two days, looking quite exquisite in her faux animal skin stretch top and black leather pants, with her long black hair wind blown. She had driven down in her brand new, bright red convertible Mercedes which she had been dying to show me. She was so excited to be out in the country and to see us again that once she started talking I didn't think she would ever stop. I didn't tell her about what was happening at the property because since she was a medium and I knew she would find it out for herself soon enough. As she was driving up to the house she felt very uneasy as if something or someone was watching here. When she walked from her car up to verandah steps she instantly felt very cold, jumped and looked around to see who it was that just touched her. She had such a look on her face when I opened the door that I was shocked.

"What's wrong?"

"It felt like someone just touch my shoulder, but when I turned around there wasn't anybody there. I felt a hand on my shoulder and it was cold, so cold that it chilled me to the bone. I have never felt like that before" she explained rubbing both of her arms to warm up, as she hesitantly she came on into the house.

After taking Jonathan into the city so he could get a taxi to the airport Natasha and I headed back home. Like two school girls we sat around in our pajamas, eating popcorn, drinking wine, catching up on the news of the old neighborhood and talking about old times, all the while Natasha kept looking over her shoulder as if someone was there. She told me that she sensed that this house has an evil presence but said that maybe it was that she was just tired and would have to explore that more in the morning. It must have been half past midnight before we finally said good night and went upstairs to our rooms to sleep.

This morning a storm had set in. I figured that we would have a good view of the property from at least three of the four sides of the verandah to watch the rain coming down and to see if any animals who might venture out in the rain to feed.

After having a leisurely breakfast in the sun room, we went into the living room where I had built a small fire in the fireplace. We sat and talked about things that happened in the city after since we have been gone. Natasha was about to tell me about Mrs. Adams old cat Tom when there was a knock on the front door. When I opened the front door there stood this man, of African American origin, who looked like he had been walking in the rain for hours. His hair was long and matted to his head, he smelled like he hadn't taken a shower in years, his clothes were muddy and wet. His eyes had the look of a crazed person. Crap, there are those cold shivers again. For some strange reason this man looked familiar but I couldn't place it under all that muck. Could he have been the person standing in the road the other night?

"May I help you?"

"My car broke down some ways back and since this was the only house I saw with lights on I made for it. May I use your telephone?"

Being the overly suspicious person that I am, I told him that I would call the garage in town to see if they could come out to help him with his car and asked him to wait on the verandah.

"Look ladies I don't want to go back out in this down pour would it be ok if I stay here until they come if you get in touch with them?" He said politely but he seemed overly anxious, almost nervous about something.

"They won't come to the house, they will only go to where your car is broken down on the road" I said rather strongly.

Natasha said "You know it is raining really hard out and he looks cold, maybe it would be best if we take him back to his car and wait there for the tow truck. He can warm up by the fire."

"It will be over an hour before they show up if I can get through to them and if they can send a truck out," I replied trying to make Natasha understand that I didn't trust this guy. "Wait here on the verandah out of the rain and I'll go call to see if and when they can come out" I said hoping that Natasha would get it this time.

When I picked up the telephone to call out, the line was dead, "Great, just great, now what am I going to do" I said silently to myself.

When I went back to the verandah the stranger wasn't there, I heard voices coming from the kitchen. Natasha and the stranger were in the kitchen. She was making sandwiches and she was pouring hot coffee for him out of my good cups.

"The least we can do is feed him and give him a cup of coffee to warm him up" she said.

"Well the telephone is dead so there won't be a tow truck coming out" I said very disgusted, especially since the stranger hadn't even wiped his muddy feet when he came in the house and tracked mud all the way to the kitchen.

After the man had finished eating Natasha suggested that we give him some dry clothes and let him rest for a while and maybe the telephone would come back on soon.

Begrudgingly, I gave him some of Jonathan's old clothes that I was going to give to Goodwill and showed him to the downstairs bathroom so he could clean up. While he was cleaning up, I took Natasha aside and said very sternly "Natasha, are you crazy letting a stranger in this house, we are alone or did that escape your mind. What if he is an ax murder or something. There have been things happening here that I can't explain so I'm really leery of letting anybody strange in my house."

She looked at me as if I was crazy so I sat her down and quickly told her some of the things that had been going on. I don't think I got through to her. I suggested that as soon as the stranger has finished cleaning up we drive him into town to the garage and let him take care of his own car.

"That might work ladies but what if the garage is closed, what will you do with me then" the stranger now clean asked as he walked into the room. He was actually nice looking once he cleaned off al that dirt. Startled that he had come in so quietly I replied "Then we could leave you at the café or the police station and they would be able to direct you to someone that could help you."

"Do you think it is wise to drive over the rain soaked road, it is bad enough when it is dry" he said?

That made me think that maybe this man wasn't a stranger but someone that lived around here for only the locals knew how the road is when it was wet or dry.

"Do you live around here?" I inquired

"My family used to several years ago but they have been away for a long time."

"Why did you come back on such a miserable day?"

"I have a special purpose for being here but I'm mainly here to check on some property that was promised to me but was left to a relative. I just wanted to see how it looked and if they were taking care of it."

" I don't know many families around here but maybe I know your family. What was the name?"

He stopped and thought for a moment then said "Martins."

"That's the family across the road, or at least that's the name on their mail box across the road. Maybe I could drive you over there and they could help you."

"They don't want to see me. I'm sort of a black sheep where they are concerned and I know that they wouldn't help me."

I was trying to think of someway, anyway to get this strange man out of my house.

"I'll check the telephone again to see if it is working now" I said hurrying out of the room.

Natasha had slipped away while I was talking to the stranger. We heard her scream from the basement and went running. We found her crumpled at the bottom of the stairs in the basement.

"Natasha, what happened? Are you all right?"

She was groggy but said "I saw a man hanging there from the rafters."

Immediately I knew whom she was talking about. The stranger had followed me down the stairs.

"Let's get her upstairs" I said.

Helping her up, she kept muttering incoherently about a man hanging there and the strange feeling like somebody else was in the room with her and had pushed her down the stairs. I would have to tell her about "him" after I got rid of the stranger because I didn't want him to know what was happening in my house. We got her into the living room where she could lie down on the couch. Covering her with a lite throw blanked, I poured her a glass of brandy to help calm her down.

"Can you watch her for a minute, I want to see if the telephone is working?" The telephone was working and I took the liberty and called the garage for a tow truck.

"Natasha are you feeling better now?" I asked upon returning to the living room.

"I saw a man hanging in your basement. He was still twitching. When I screamed, he vanished and it felt like someone pushed me down the stairs. I felt hands on my back. I know that I'm a medium and I have seen things in dreams before but I have never seen something so vividly, they usually have always been just flashes of things."

"Just lie back and rest for now" I said flashing a quick look at the stranger. She understood and laid back down on the couch. I told the man that I had called the tow truck company.

"The tow truck will be here soon. Can you give me a lift to my car and I'll wait for them there" he said?

"Let me get my keys and we'll be off."

The rain was stopping as I drove the stranger to his car. Leaving hin there I hurried back to the house. I wasn't gone but 10 minutes or so and when I returned to the house Natasha wasn't on the couch. I called out to her. She answered from upstairs. When I finally found her, she was in the guest room over looking the cemetery.

"Jonathan's family cemetery?" she inquired.

"Yes, most of them at least, what are you doing up, I think you should go lie back down for a while" I replied.

"I'm all right. I'd like to go down there when the ground is drier. If that, is ok with you?" she asked.

"Sure, I go in there all the time. Now as to the person you saw hanging in the basement. That was Jonathan's great-uncle Zachary. The story goes he was in love with a young slave girl and wanted to marry her but Nathaniel, that's Jonathan's great-grandfather, forbid it and had her sent away. When Zachary found out, she had been sent to slave traders he and Nathaniel argued. He later found out by way of the underground railroad that she was with child. Thinking it was his child he became very distraught. She had been killed for trying to escape by the slave trader because she refused his advances. He went crazy, nothing or nobody could console him and he hung himself here in the basement."

"Wow. He must have loved her a lot for his spirit to still be "hanging" around in this old house " she said with a very concerned look on her face.

I didn't hear the second part of her sentence because I was too busy wondered if today was the anniversary of his death because I hadn't seen him or felt him before.

"I'm sorry Natasha what did you say? Do you think that today could have been the anniversary of his death? Maybe that is why you saw him" I said anticipating her to say yes but she just shock her head and shrugged her shoulders.

"You know you never got that man's name" she said changing the subject.

I didn't want to know his name, that's why I didn't ask him I thought to myself.

"I need to tell you more about the house."

"No, I want to find out things about this house myself" as

she started sensing the room. As we went room by room to see what, if anything she felt, she stopped and told me that she needed a note pad so she could write down her impressions and feelings. When we walked into the small pink room, which was Constance's room from what I have been told, she said that there was sadness in the room and a cold spot here. Said that we should come back again over the course of the next few days to see if anything transpires.

When she came with me into our bedroom she immediately felt cold, her throat started tightening and said that she couldn't come in.

"The lady of the house still resides in this room."

"How can you tell did something horrible happen in here" I asked?

"This was the Nathaniel and Angela's bedroom when Jonathan's great-grandfather was alive, right? He was a horrible man doing things to that were unspeakable. This is the most hated room in the whole house from what I have felt."

"Can you see anything?"

"I feel the hatred in this room. I'm not getting any visions right now maybe it is best that we come back in here at night. It probably would be the best time to sense the "hot spot of hate. I want to go outside and get some air."

With that we went outside to the back porch where we could look on the woods behind the house. The sun had come out and everything smelled so fresh. After a while I fixed lunch which we ate peacefully on the back verandah.

After lunch Natasha said "Let's go to the woods out there." I told her that the field was extremely muddy and it would be best that we wait until it has a chance to dry out a little.

"Hey, let's go into town, I know of this great antique store that you would just love."

Our drive into town was uneventful, Natasha oohed and aahed at the different things we saw on the way. She was quite taken with our small town, she even suggested that one day she might like to try living in a small town, then gave a giggle after saying it, for we both knew that she was a big city girl born and bred. We explored the antique store for what seemed like hours buying all sorts of "needful things" or at least we thought they were. It was almost five when we finish and I suggested that we go to the Orange Blossom Café for dinner before we head back home. Our waitresses, Sally was a cordial as ever taking our order and checking on us during our meal, even smiling once or twice. We were both tired on the way home so we didn't talk too much except for the fact that we were both glad that the stranger's car hadn't been there on the road again

"Oh boy, I hope he doesn't come back tonight, I don't think I can handle that weirdo again." I complained.

Natasha piped up "If he does come back, I'll throw him out on his ear." We both laughed at that.

There was no sign of him when we drove up to the house. I did notice that the front door was ajar. "Look. The front doors open."

We crept up the front steps hoping that if anybody was inside they wouldn't hear us. But if they were inside for sure they would have heard our car drive up.

"I'll get to the telephone and call the sheriff once we get in" I told Natasha.

"I check the downstairs rooms" Natasha whispered.

"Hello, Sheriff this is Amy Chamberlain out at Heavenly Acres I would like to report a break in and the he may still be here", I said as quietly as possible. Natasha returned before I finished speaking to the sheriff's office and said that there wasn't anybody in this part of the house.

"The sheriff will send a car right out and they said that we should not continue searching the house for who knows who or what we might find, so let's go back outside and wait for the sheriff to show up."

It wasn't very long before Deputy David Long showed up. While he was checking the inside, Dr. Jefferson drove up the drive. As he jumped out of the car, he called "Amy are you all right? The Martin's from across the street called me when the saw the patrol car pulling in".

"When we got home from town, the front door was open and since there have been strange things going on I called the sheriff's office immediately" I said regretting it as soon as it came out.

"What strange things? How come you didn't tell me, I would have come over to check things out while Jonathan was gone."

"Doctor strange things have been happening even when Jonathan is home but he doesn't believe me when I tell him or try to tell him about them."

The deputy came out letting me know that there wasn't anybody in the house but he was going to check the out buildings just to be sure that there wasn't anybody out there hiding. The doctor went along to help.

"Natasha I'm cold, let's go in and get warmed up."

"I'm all for that" she said rubbing her arms. I put on a pot of water for some tea and suggested that Natasha go up and take a hot shower to get warmed up.

"I'm not going to miss a thing that's going on. I'll wait until after everybody's gone before I go up stairs."

"Natasha there's nothing going on, maybe I didn't latch the front door closed all the way when we left and maybe that is why it was open when we got home, could you please start a fire in the fireplace" I tried to down play my anxiety. The deputy and Dr. Jefferson returned stating that they couldn't find anybody. The deputy said that if anything else happens to call and they would be right out. With that he left his card and said good night. Dr. Jefferson, on the other hand, decided that he was going to stay to be sure that nothing happened.

"Doctor, we are all right. We really don't need a babysitter." I said, not wanting him to stay because I just didn't trust him still.

"Oh, Amy let him stay. It will be nice to have somebody

besides you to talk to. Maybe he can tell me about this old house and the two of us can go exploring as he tells me about it" Natasha said quite girlishly. If I didn't know better, I would say that Natasha was flirting with the good doctor.

Over cups of hot, steaming tea Dr. Jefferson told Natasha some of the things he knew about the house and property. He, thankfully, left out the part about Jonathan's great-grandfather being a beast and the corpse we found. I explained to him that Natasha knew about Zachary and that she thought she saw him in the basement the other day. Natasha explained to the doctor that she was a psychic/medium and that she had never experienced seeing things so real like that before and it really scared her and refused to go back down there unless a big strong man goes down there with her. With that I left the room so they could "talk."

Chapter 6

When I cam downstairs the next morning I heard singing in the kitchen. Natasha and the doctor seemed to be a very cozy toward each other, smiling and giggling like school kids. It was kind of weird seeing my best friend and the "doctor" as a couple. Did he stay last night? That really gave me shivers. Where did he stay?

"Are you cold, Amy?" the doctor asked handing me a cup of coffee.

"No I just had a strange thought. Thank you for the coffee. What's for breakfast?" I asked trying to change the subject really fast.

"I whipped up egg's benedict, hash browns, home made biscuits with strawberry jam to go with it and lots of hot coffee. How's that sound?"

"Delish" I said filling my plate.

"Well what should we do today, Natasha?" I was trying to

direct my question to her so that she would know that I didn't want the doctor to stay.

"Frank and I are going to go over to his property so that he can "show" me around." "Oh, ok, can I expect you back by lunch or dinner?" With a quick look and a wink at the doctor Natasha said "Dinner."

Conversation was light during breakfast. I told Natasha to go get ready for the day and I would take care of things. She must have been on cloud nine because I don't think her feet hit the ground once. The doctor helped clean up after breakfast. I didn't talk much other than about the weather and I hoped they had a good day. Natasha came busting in the room all dressed up like she was going to a spring picnic, I told her that she should take a coat because the afternoons are starting to get cool. With that they went out the door hand in hand. I felt like I was sending her out like she was my daughter on her first date. Sighing, I went about my daily chores.

The walk to the mail box was nice, air was so fresh, there was still a slight smell of rain lingering but it sure was a pleasant smell, the birds singing and there was nobody strange to bother me.

"Hello, neighbor" someone called from behind me. When I turned around it was a lady standing by her mail box across the road.

"Hello" I replied. From a distance the lady seemed as if she was one hundred years old but as I got closer her appearance changed to a pleasant looking lady, I would say in her lat 60's.

"Hi, I'm Annette Martin. You must be Mrs. Chamberlain, Jonathan's wife."

"Yes, I am and please call me Amy."

"Would you like to come up to the house for coffee? I just made an apple coffee cake and would love to have someone to share it with"

"Yes, thank you. My husband it out of town on business and my friend that is staying with me went to Dr. Jefferson's house for the day. I would love to, by the way thank you for calling Dr. Jefferson last night, I thought that somebody had broken into the house but I must not have latched it shut because the door was ajar when we got home."

"That must have been an awful fright, if you ever need anybody to come over please give us a call. I'll give you our number when we get into the house" she said very politely.

The Martin house was small but very cozy from what I could see because we came in the back door into the kitchen. The living room was next to the kitchen and I could hear someone in there but didn't ask. I explained that Jonathan's grandmother left the property to him and that was the only reason that we were here.

"You must be all a twitter going through that old house, exploring the rooms and living there. There is so much room and land. I would give anything just to go to the front verandah."

"Would you and your family like to come over for lunch or dinner sometime?" I asked.

"Oh, my husband wouldn't hear of that. You see he doesn't have much to do with neighbors, he keeps to himself mostly and asks that I do so too. I'm not good at that for I love to have company."

"Did you know any of the family that lived here before we came?"

"I knew Jonathan's family when the boys were kids. They would come over and play with my son once in a while. But always left before my husband came home because he didn't like our son playing with city kids. Said it would give him the wrong idea about life."

The coffee cake was so good that it almost melted in my mouth. "You'll have to give me the recipe for this. It's great." She must have anticipated my asking because she pulled a recipe card out of her apron pocket and handed it to me, her telephone number was on the back.

"The secret to the recipe is the apples. You have to use

Granny Smith's, anything else and the flavor wouldn't be so good" she beamed.

Right about that time a large built tall man with an unshaven face and bushy sandy blonde hair came into the kitchen from the basement, startling me when he said in a rather loud voice "Who are you?" He looked as if he was once a very striking man when he was younger. He was carrying a very large meat cleaver and had on this oversized apron that was covered in blood.

I stood up and reluctantly held out my hand "Hello, I'm Amy Chamberlain, Jonathan Chamberlain's wife."

He refused my hand. Annette looked at me and just shook her head, I could sense that she was afraid of him. I definitely had the feeling that he did not want me there. I remembered the stranger from a few days ago.

"Mr. Martin a few days ago a man came to my door. He was one of your relatives but his of color. He said he has been away for a while. I thought it was strange that he came to my house and not over here. He said he was here checking on a piece of property that was supposed to be left to him but wasn't. I told him he should come over here too asked about it but made excuses as to why he couldn't come over. He never told me his name and I was wondering if he ever made it over here."

"Nobody has come over here and I don't have any relatives." He replied.

I took that as my cue to leave, so I made the excuse that I had some food cooking and had to get back to it, said my good byes and left. I looked back as I was walking down the drive and saw Mr. Martin standing in the window with this hateful look on his face and it made me wonder what happened that made him that way.

Instead of going back to the house I decided since it was warm and the sun was shining, I'd go out to the little brook and sit there for a while to enjoy the scenery. While sitting there I was so relaxed I fell asleep. I must have been asleep for hours because it was almost dark when I woke up. While walking back to the house I had this strange feeling that I shouldn't be apprehensive about going inside anymore. Why? I couldn't figure that one out.

Natasha and the doctor showed up around seven that night, all smiles and giggles again. I'm glad Natasha is happy, but I'm still cautious about the doctor. We used the grand dining room for dinner and it was delightful this evening. It was great to have people in the house, it made it seem like I was at home here. I wished that Jonathan could have joined us but his business seemed to keep him away from home so much more now that ever before. Ok, don't start thinking of weird things now, it is only business.

"Tomorrow we will all go over to my place and have an old-fashioned picnic, my housekeeper keeps telling me that I should have you over and now is as good a time as any, what do you say?" the doctor asked.

Since I was very curious about where he lived I agreed and said that I would bring a special bottle of wine from our cellar.

The next day the sun was shining, the birds singing, it was nice and warm, perfect day for a picnic I thought. I asked Natasha to come to the cellar with me to pick out a bottle of wine forgetting about her experience down there.

"I really don't want to go down there. I'm getting vibrations from there that someone or something doesn't want me down there."

"It will be all right Natasha. We will go down slow and I'll turn on all the lights so there won't be any dark spots. Here I'll even take this very large, heavy candle stick with us so if we do see a ghost I can smack it with it." We both laughed at that knowing that you can't smack a ghost.

"There is something that I really would like to show you but if you don't want to see it . . . "

"Ok, ok, I'll go" she said pretending that she wasn't scared.

Slowly we descended down the cellar steps, the boards

creaking under the hour weight. I made some creepy noises and Natasha smacked me on the shoulder "Don't do that!".

When all the lights were on in the cellar, it wasn't a bad place since the remodeling. All the wine racks and shelves were on one wall and there was a work bench on another wall. Boxes and crates stood against one wall and the wall where the door to the tunnel was on the other. Natasha asked where the door went to.

"That's the underground slave tunnel where runaway slaves stayed until it was safe enough for them to escape. It's kind of creepy down there. The only lighting there is, are oil lamps. You can go in there if you want but take this oil can with you because I think the lamps are out of oil."

"Does Frank know about the tunnel?" she asked.

"Yeah, he told us some stories about it. Nothing juicy happened in there. It's just a tunnel where the slave stayed."

"Where does it go to?"

"To the barn, I guess they were loaded into wagons and transported out from there."

I wondered if I should take red or white wine and decided to take one of each just to be on the safe side, I surely didn't want to offend the good doctor since he and Natasha were on first name basis now.

When we arrived at the doctor's house a little before noon, Natasha tole me that this house has many spirits living here also but they are warm and friendly spirts, not like the ones that live at my house. It was an amazing house, the long paved drive leading up to the house was lined with very well manicured bushes with a pond that was almost the length of the drive with four fountains of sea sculptures of various sizes and shapes. The house made me feel as if I was in a European castle, it was humongous, it looked like it went on forever. Now this really made me feel like Dracula was going to come swooping down and bite my neck, thank god it was day time. When we finally reached the massive front door, the housekeeper was waiting for us. I started to ask her to elaborate more about the ghosts/spirits that live at my house but the front door opened and there stood this bright and cheery lady.

"Hello, my name is Eleanora, you can call me Nora, you must be Amy and Natasha. The doctor is so looking forward to today."

She reminded me of *Mrs. Doubtfire* by the way she said hel-looooo. She is a very pleasant looking older lady with her greying hair tied up in a bun, like a grand motherly type. She was wearing Scandinavian style clothing. Shaking our hands and showing us in the house, she never stopped talking about how please she was that the doctor was having company and how she was so please she could finally fix a meal for more than one person. She showed us to a large living room furnished with overstuffed white couches and chairs. After pouring us drinks and telling us that the doctor would be down in a few minutes, she vanished through a door. I guessed it must lead back to the kitchen somehow. We took our drinks and waited for the doctor on the balcony. The balcony over looked more ponds with fountains, manicured lawns, marvelous flower gardens and a very large gazebo in the very middle of it all.

From the living room you could see the dining room. The table was set with the finest crystal and china I had ever seen. It looked as if it was so fragile that if you touched it, it would break.

When the doctor came into the room, he looked more like Count Dracula than ever before with his formal wear and ascot. Dracula only came out a night so I guess I'm safe for now but what about after dark? Does he have his cohorts waiting in the basement? To break the tension that was building, I commented about the crystal and china.

"It has been in my family for more than 100 years. I only use it when I have the occasion to entertain. It was imported from Switzerland. I have several Tiffany lamps from there also in the house. I just love the old things."

I'll bet, I thought to myself. I still don't know why I don't trust him but I still don't. Lunch was marvelous and afterward we took a stroll through the gardens. I was glad to walk around for lunch made me sleepy and one thing I don't want to do is sleep here! The doctor insisted that I call him Frank for we are good neighbors now and he would like that. Upon arriving back at the house Frank asked us if we would like to have the grand tour of the inside of the house. He said that most of the things in the house are the original furnishings. It was a miracle that they survived the Civil War, but they did. His house was much larger than ours, I thought that we would get lost for all the corridors and rooms that we were in but Frank said that he knew this place like the back of his hand. The one room that he had to show us was the library. There were books in there from the 1600's. All of them original. Of course they were all in locked glass cases to protect them from the elements. He said that his collection was worth more than he could ever in his wildest dreams imagine. He got sad when he talked about the house because he was the last of his family and had no one to leave any of this to. I asked him why he never married.

"I was married once but she passed away before they could start a family and since I loved her so much I never thought about remarrying again. That's enough of that. I didn't ask you two here to become melancholy. Let's go down stairs and dance in the grand ballroom."

With that he turned to Natasha, whisking her around the room led the way to the grand ballroom.

It was a grand day and when we returned home Jonathan was waiting for us.

"Where have you two been? You look like two school girls just back from vacation."

"We have a wonderful day with Dr. Jefferson. Oh, Jonathan his property is twice the size of ours and that house. I thought we would get lost. It was so big. You'll have to come with me some time and see it for yourself." I said breathlessly. "By the way it's good to have you home again" I added with a light kiss on his cheek.

"The merger went faster than I thought so I came home early to surprise the two of you with a dinner in the big city, but I guess since you're so ecstatic from your day, dinner will have to wait until tomorrow."

"Jonathan" Natasha started "Would it be ok if I asked Frank to come over for drinks tonight?"

I remembered about the colleague that Dr. Jefferson wanted to bring over and thought this was as good as any to ask.

"Let's have a quite night tonight. I think he may need to relax from his trip. We can have Dr. Morgan over tomorrow, ok?"

"I'm going to be having to go back to the city soon and I don't want to waste one minute" Natasha said frowning quite childishly.

Jonathan went to bed early and after I knew he was asleep I slipped downstairs noiselessly to call Dr. Jefferson to let him know Jonathan was home. After agreeing to call his colleague and see us for drinks tomorrow evening I slipped back in bed. Jonathan was resting so peacefully he didn't wake up even when I tripped on the bed post stubbing my toe and crying out in pain.

We were woken up by screaming. It came from Natasha's room. Reaching her door, we came across a ghastly sight. Natasha was standing in the middle of the room. The wind was twirling around her like a cyclone.

"Natasha, reach for my hand" Jonathan called to her. Fighting as hard as he could he reached in the room. The wind was so strong I pushed against his back to help get him into the room. Just as her finger tips touched his the wind stopped and she fell to the floor.

"Natasha, are you all right" I cried as I dashed across the room, grasping her in my arms. Jonathan brought her a glass of water and handed it to her.

"What in the world was going on in here" we asked at the same time.

"I don't know I got up because I heard sobbing sounds and I thought it was coming from the room next door but when I got in the middle of the room the wind started whirling around me and wouldn't stop."

"See, Jonathan, I told you that strange things were happening here and you wouldn't believe me" I said looking straight in his face. "I'll stay in here with you for the rest of the night Natasha and that way maybe we can protect each other" I added. Then remembering the incident in the basement. "Jonathan, Natasha had an encounter also in the basement. She said that she saw your uncle hanging from the rafters." Jonathan just looked at me in disbelief.

"Amy have you been filling her head with all of your little fantasies?"

"I want to leave here before something else happens" Natasha said weakly.

"Natasha, let Amy stay here with you for the rest of the night, when morning comes if you still feel the same way, I'll help you pack." He replied angrily.

"I won't be able to sleep, I'm going down stairs and make myself a cup of tea, are you coming Amy?" Natasha asked as she pushed her way past Jonathan.

"I'll be right down" I replied. After Natasha left the room I turned to Jonathan "I told you. I think it is time we have someone come here and see if this place is haunted."

"Don't be ridiculous. You're just delusional. Natasha is a psychic and they have things like this happens to them all the time. " Jonathan said storming out of the room.

Frustrated I joined Natasha in the kitchen.

"Natasha, listen. Dr. Jefferson is coming over tomorrow with his colleague that he told us about. Will you stay at least until he has a chance to talk to Jonathan?" I asked. "Just until" Natasha said staring into her cup of tea.

The following morning Dr. Jefferson called to let me know that his friend was in town and wanted me to come over so I could talk to him and tell him everything that has been happening so he would have some idea what he was up against. I made excuses that I was going to visit a neighbor lady who lives down the road to Jonathan and Natasha and I headed toward Dr. Jefferson's house by way of the back road. I hated lying to Jonathan but I had to do something to make him listen. After spending about a half hour explaining things to Dr. Harry Thomas, we left him to digest all that was told to him. Dr. Jefferson asked Natasha to stay on for a while and if she felt uncomfortable staying with us that she could stay with him. She told him that she would stay but wanted to stay with me to protect me. Who is going to protect who?

The next day I invited Dr. Jefferson and Dr. Thomas over for lunch, knowing that it would make Natasha and Jonathan happy that I was extending my house to Dr. Jefferson. Even though I was starting to warm up to Dr. Jefferson, there was still something about him I didn't trust.

Dr. Thomas introduced himself simply as Harry a good friend of Dr. Jefferson that he was very interested the history of the old south, old houses and such. He asked Jonathan to show him around the estate. Jonathan (the proud peacock) strutted around showing him this and that and just about everything a person could see in an afternoon.

While they were walking Harry asked Jonathan if he noticed anything out of the ordinary happening around the estate, such as manifestations.

"I don't believe in those things so why would I see them?"

"I was just wondering. I bet you get weird feelings sometimes when you are out in the cemetery?"

Jonathan stopped and looked at him like he was crazy. "No, I don't but my wife, who has a very vivid imagination, says she does."

"Really?" Harry said, scratching his chin looking at me, boy

I'm glad Jonathan didn't see him wink at me. "I have heard that old houses sometimes take on the personality of its former owners, I'm fascinated with old houses and their history, maybe sometime you would share yours with me?" Jonathan wasn't getting the drift of what the doctor was trying to get at.

"I have some friends who are paranormal investigators. They would really enjoy the opportunity of coming here just to have a look around. Would you allow me to call them?"

"There's nothing here!" Jonathan yelled. "Now if you don't mind, if you want to still look around, please stop talking about such things."

"Ok" the doctor said looking at us shrugging his shoulders.

Later that afternoon when I was saying goodbye to the doctors, I inquired, "What do you think?"

"Well, he is in denial that there is anything happening here. I would like to go out to the stone circle area and have a look around."

"I was walking out there one day and found this path leading from the stone circle to the back road which leads to Dr. Jefferson's house, you could use that path and Jonathan would never know you were there."

Dr. Thomas said that he would like to have his friends come out anyway just to look at the stone circle. They could pretend that they are neighbors that live down the road and maybe I could have them over for dinner or something. I thought that was a good idea and told him it would be best to do so in a hurry because I didn't think I could stand much more of this old house. With that they said goodby and went on their way. While Jonathan was in the house Natasha and I walked around in the cemetery talking about what we should do next. She told me that the spirits in the cemetery were telling her that we had to move quickly because something was about to happen and it was not going to be good.

That night the house seemed to go mad. This time Jonathan

heard and saw what I had been trying to tell him all along. Things started moving by themselves, we heard whispering voices then high pitched screams, the lights went on and off, the water turned on and off, cold bursts of air would whip through the room, loud pounding on the doors and walls, very loud footsteps coming and going and the fireplace even blasted out flames then died down. All we could do was hope that who every or whatever it was would calm down soon. The most frightening of all was when we went to bed, our bed started shaking violently, then this glowing figure appeared hovering over at the end of the bed. It started to take on a shape but Jonathan through a pillow at it and it vanished.

"Now you see what I have been talking about" I said to him as I hunkered down under the covers. "Now can we please have a paranormal investigator come?"

Defiantly he said "No!"

"Why not" I said very angry.

"Because this is just a figment of your imagination and/or it is some kind of hypnosis that you have created this for Natasha's sake".

I couldn't believe my ears "Oh, wake up and smell the ghosts, there is something happening here and it is getting worse. We have to do something about it and now!"

"Old houses have ghosts, if I believed in that sort of thing, which I don't, and this one is no exception. They just have to learn to live with us because I am not going to move or be run out of here or have a bunch of ghost busters around here. Now go to sleep". Yeah, right, go to sleep, I don't think so. I laid awake for a long time before I finally gave in and fell into a fitful sleep.

The door slammed shut. I was in total darkness, all of the sudden something pushed me to the floor. "Stay down woman" it bellowed. Quivering and scared to the point of not being able to catch my breath, I reached out, trying to feel for the person that pushed me. I crawled on the floor afraid to get up. Feeling the air not touching anything I squeaked out "Who are you?" No answer.

It is so cold in here. I could feel dirt under my knees, I decided that I would at least try to find a wall to pull myself up on. I had a feeling that I was in the tunnel and knew that there were oil lamps on the walls but I didn't have any matches, so I tried hard to see if there was any light coming from anywhere. Finally finding the walls and standing up slowly just in case I was pushed down again. I slowly adjusted to the dark. I did see a very faint light coming from down the tunnel. I slowly made my way down the tunnel toward the light, tripping on things in the floor that hadn't been there before when Jonathan and I were down here or at least I didn't remember them being here. A very cold light breeze was coming from somewhere.

The light was getting a little brighter and I heard voices but couldn't make them out. I wish Jonathan was here with me. I reached a door in the tunnel that was here before. I stood at the door afraid to go in and tried to hear what was going on inside. There were two distinct male voices. I thought I recognized Jonathan's voice and almost cried out but thought better. I put my ear to the door making sure that it didn't move. I could just barely make out what they were saying.

"We have to do it tonight" on voice said.

"I know but we have t make it look like it was an accident. We don't want to put any suspicion on ourselves" the other voice said. "I have waited for this a long time and I am not waiting any longer".

"Calm down and be patient. I have the plan all in place now and if it all goes the way I planned it will be all over by morning".

My heart sank and I felt sick. Should I burst into the room and tell them that the jig is up or should I wait to see what they have planned and foil their plan? I had to get out of there so I turned around and made my way back down the tunnel and to the basement door. The door pushed open with great ease. The fresh air really felt good in my lungs.

I ran up the stairs to my bedroom and wondered if I should call Dr. Jefferson. Was he in on the plot? Should I call Mrs. Martin to see if someone could come over and stay with me? Should I tell Natasha and have her call the police and have hem come out? But what would she tell them, would they really believe that there was a plot to do away with me? Was it me that they were plotting against? I wish I had bought a gun to protect myself.

I decided to call Dr. Jefferson's house just to see if he was there because there was no way he could have gotten home by the time I got out of the tunnel, up the stairs and to my room. The phone rang, one, two, three, four, five, then "Hello" it was the housekeeper.

"Eleanora, hi, it's Amy, is Dr. Jefferson home? I quietly asked making sure that nobody heard me.

"No, Mrs. Chamberlain, he said he was going to your house and wouldn't be back for sometime. Why hasn't he shown up? Oh, my I hope nothing has happened to him. Should I call the police to have them check?"

"No, I'm sure that he is with Jonathan and they haven't come in the house yet. I think I see his car in the drive. I've been in the attic and didn't know he was here, thank you" with that I hung up and sunk to the floor sobbing.

It was getting dark out and my fears began to rise when I heard Jonathan calling my name from downstairs. I wondered did he put a trip wire on the stairs and wants me to fall going down the stairs or is he going to poison me with something that Dr. Jefferson has given him? Will Dr. Jefferson do an autopsy on me and tell everybody that I died from natural causes? My heart was racing so that I could hardly breath. I had to act natural, act like I didn't know anything about the plot I had over heard. I had to get out of the house, run away, go back to the city.

"Amy, where are you" Jonathan called even closer now. Pretend you were in the bathroom, quick run some hot water, splash your face, grab a towel, turn on the radio.

"Hi, honey I was calling you, didn't you hear me?" Jonathan asked as he stood at the bathroom door.

"I'm sorry, I was washing my face and didn't hear you." I said turning the water and the radio off.

"I have a surprise waiting for you downstairs" he said encircling me with his strong arms. I had to pretend I didn't know anything at least until I could get downstairs and out the front door.

We started toward the stairs. I searched the stairs for any signs of a trip wire but didn't see anything. As we walked down the stairs I carefully took each step to be sure. Jonathan looked at me with a questioning look on his face. "Just a little stiff, I did some aerobics today and I'm sore" I said trying to throw him off.

When we got downstairs it was dark but the dining room had an eerie glow coming from it. I didn't want to go in there but Jonathan held the door for me. What I saw took my breath away, he had put a king size bed in the living room, there were lit candles all around and soft music was playing. He gently picked me up and laid me on the bed.

"Oh babe, I've wanted to do this ever since we moved in here."

He started kissing me and rubbing me all over. How could I refuse such a wonderful offer. The kissing turned into biting and his arms were crushing me. What is going on? "Jonathan" I said you're hurting me". No response the biting got worse and no matter how hard I struggled to get away he wouldn't let me go. "Jonathan, let me go, you're hurting me. Are you crazy!" I screamed.

"Amy, Amy wake up you're having a bad dream". I opened my eyes and I find that I'm confined to a very tight area. I felt around and found that the walls were wooden, I couldn't get up, I realized that I was in a box. A small window opened up above my eyes and I could see Jonathan standing on a dirt ledge above the box.

"Ashes to ashes. Dust to dust" was bing said as dirt started hitting the box. The first dirt that hit the wind panicked me. I started kicking, screaming and clawing the box to let Jonathan know that I was alive in this box and not to put any more dirt on it, but he must not have heard me. All went dark, knowing that I had been buried alive, I could hear my heart pounding in my chest and head. It was getting heard to breath, it was so hot, I am starting to sweat, I'm gasping for breath, tears start running down my face. I finally decide that I have lost and I have to give in, I'm going to die. I lay here waiting for the last breath to be taken out of my body.

The next thing I know I'm in my own bed, lying next to Jonathan.

"Babe, you so hot can you move over" Jonathan said as he was rolling over. I laid there wondering what was going on. Somebody or something is trying to tell me that they want me dead. I know I'm not crazy but somehow I have to find a way to stop this.

Morning came and I was so tired all I wanted to do was stay in bed but Jonathan announced he was going into town and if us girls wanted to come along we had bettered get a move on. Knowing that Dr. Thomas's paranormal team was coming in today, I told him that I had made a lunch date with a lady friend down the road, but that if Natasha wanted to go, she was welcome to go.

"Hey, you're getting to be quite the socialite, making all these new friends, you'll have to have a dinner party and invite all of them over so I can meet them to" he said quite cheerfully. That was great now I had an excuse to really bring them over. My plans are starting to come together.

After Jonathan and Natasha left I went to the cellar to pick up a nice bottle of wine for lunch and was confronted with a dark figure standing at the door to the tunnel. He dashed into the tunnel trying to hide from me. I yelled at it but it didn't stop. Instead of going back upstairs and calling the police, or Dr. Jefferson, I stupidly followed it into the tunnel, forgetting what I had heard the day before. I grabbed a flashlight on my way in. I started to run but thought better of it for it could be waiting for me in any of the side tunnels. So, slowly I crept checking each side tunnel as I went. Almost to the end of the tunnel I found nothing. I didn't want to go up the old ladder to the barn knowing that there could still be bodies buried in there but I like a fool started up the ladder. All of the sudden something grabbed my legs and pulled me down. I hit so hard I blacked out. Next thing I know I'm back in my bed covered in dirt not knowing how I got there. I tried setting up but my head hurt so bad I had to lay back down for a few more minutes. I heard a car drive up and slowly got out of bed and went to the window. Dr. Thomas and four other people as they were getting out. I gingerly went down the stairs and met them at the front door. Gasps were all I heard before I passed out.

Dr. Jefferson was bending over me holding smelling salts. What an awful odor, it really made me cough and each time I did my head throbbed.

"What happened to you?" He asked.

"I saw this figure down in the cellar and I ran after it when it went into the tunnel. I started climbing the ladder at the end of the tunnel and was yanked off the ladder, hitting my head when I fell".

'You might have a slight concussion, you had bettered stay laying down for a while. Where is Jonathan?" Dr. Jefferson asked.

"He went to town and should be back any time now, I think."

"While your husband is away I'll have my team start looking around. As soon as you hear a car get back here on the double. Do you guys understand?" The four strangers nodded their heads and off they went. I started to get up but Dr. Jefferson wouldn't let me.

"I said stay down for a while. I know where things are and I'll help myself if I need or want anything".

"Ok" I replied weakly. The team returned before Jonathan came home and were busily telling the doctors what they had found. I stayed put on the couch while Dr. Jefferson was handing me aspirins and water, I was thinking that if they wanted me to know what they found they would tell me.

After a while I felt well enough to clean up before Jonathan and Natasha got home. Once they got home all talking about what they had found stopped and everybody acted like they were just there socially. Dr. Thomas told me in private that he would talk to me about the findings later. Finally I was introduced to the "parapsychological team". Jason, he handles all the equipment, Mark, is our resident clairvoyant and helps with the equipment, Shelly, is a psychic and Tina is a medium. I wondered if when they first arrived if they experienced what Natasha did. The afternoon went very well and they stayed on into evening, when he had a nice barbeque. Everybody was really enjoying themselves. About 10 p.m. everybody called it a night, piled into Dr. Jefferson's car and left. My head was starting to really pound again and I told Jonathan that I was very tried and went up to bed. While taking a shower there was that darn shadow again. This time I ignored it, when all of the sudden the curtain flew open and there was Jonathan wearing nothing but a smile. Needless to say my headache went away real fast.

Chapter 7

One night I was awakened by Natasha standing at the side of my bed. "Shsss, follow me" was all she said. I followed her into her room. Closing the door very quietly so as to not wake anybody else up Natasha pointed to the window.

"Look, out in the stand of trees, there is a fire going. There isn't a moon tonight, let's sneak down there and see what is going on".

We dressed quickly and made our way through the field, it was tough going with no light, stumbling, and tripping we finally got across the field and headed into the trees. We could hear chanting in the distance and as quietly as we could made our way to the stone circle clearing. To our surprise there were several people there all dressed in long white gowns with hoods. There was a pig of some kind tied up close to the stone altar. The pig had flowers all around its neck like a necklace. The figures were dancing around the pig and throwing flowers on the ground around it. There was one figure dressed in a red gown that seemed to be the leader. What ever he said the others chanted along. They had a large fire going in the fire pit. All of the sudden they all dropped their robes and were dancing around in the nude. I could tell that there were 6 women and 7 men including the leader. They were passing a large goblet around and everyone was holding it up to the sky, saying something and then drinking from it. It was passed to all and then the leader. Once he drank from the goblet all dancing and chanting stopped. He said something poured some of the liquid on the pig, who squealed very loud. One of the men held up a chicken by its feet. Passing it from one to another they held the chicken up and the after all held it the leader took. He said some words, placed it on the stone altar and then cut off its head. The others started chanting and swaying back and forth as the chicken's body rolled all over the stone altar. After it finally stopped, one by one, they all went to the altar and smeared the chicken's blood on their bodies.

I started feeling sick watching this but Natasha was fascinated. She said that we just had to go to the altar after they left so that she could feel for vibrations. It didn't appeal to me but if that is what she wanted to do, I couldn't stop her. It wasn't long before the group put their robes back on, put the pig in a cage and they all left. The fire was almost out and Natasha wanted to get to it before it went out so she could see what it was that they were burning. She said that this is the way she could get a psychic view as to what was being done and what was said.

When she felt it was safe we moved in among the stones. First she touched the altar. She had a tape recorder with her and was talking into it. She sat on the ground where the pig had been and spoke into the recorder. Touching each and every one of the stones gave her more to talk about, to the recorder not to me. When I asked a question, she would just hold her finger to her lips and indicated to me to not speak right then. I got tired of watching this and moved closer to the fire because it was a little chilly. I looked into the fire and what I saw took my breath away.

"Natasha you had bettered look at this" I said quietly. Again the finger to the lips.

"Natasha you had bettered look at this" I said again a louder. She rolled her eyes and came to look at what I was pointing at. It was bones, human bones. I though she was going to faint because she had to grab onto a stone to keep from falling down.

"I am going to call the sheriff" I said, turning and heading toward home.

"No!" she yelled, then turned quickly to see if anybody had heard her. "Amy, this is not something the sheriff would understand".

"No, I don't understand. How could anybody do that?" I said almost in tears.

Just then we heard a car drive up and two males voices. We dove for cover. They were carrying shovels and buckets. They put out the last of the fire and scooped out the bones, shaking off the ashes.

"I think the ritual went well tonight. I don't think anybody will miss those old bones we dug up at the cemetery, do you?"

"We covered up our tracks pretty good, those college kids really got a kick out of that phony ritual stuff we dished out, didn't they?" They both laughed and then with buckets in hand went back to their car and drove off.

"Now I know I'm going to report this to the sheriff. Digging up bones from a cemetery is a crime" I said adamantly.

"Go ahead but who are you going to say did it, how are you going to prove it. Do you want the sheriff coming out here and looking around the altar. They probably would have you tear it down. Do you want that?" Natasha rebutted.

"I know you're right but that makes me so mad".

"We had bettered get back to the house before anybody misses us" Natasha said pulling me along.

A couple of days Jonathan had to go on another business trip only this time he asked me to come along. Boy did I hate to say no. He looked at me as if I was crazy.

"I though with all that is going on in this house you would be the first out the door. What has changed?"

"You know Natasha is still here and I can't leave her along besides the ladies down the road asked us to help with canning and we promised them we would help. If that's ok?"

"Sure, maybe this is what you needed to get your mind off of this house and the GHOOOOSTS" he said trying to make the word sound eerie. "I ain't afraid of no ghosts" he said as he tried to slime me with a kiss. I was almost overly anxious to have him leave and I think Jonathan sensed something was up but didn't say anything. He said he would only be gone a couple of days as he was walking out the door.

No sooner had he driven down the driveway than I was on the phone calling Dr. Jefferson to let him know that Jonathan was gone and they had two days freedom in the house and the grounds.

The team came right over and stared in the basement telling me that they found extreme vibrations in there. I was told that I should not tell the team anything that has and/or had happened that the team would explore and them come back and let us know if they found anything. Tina who had been in the tunnel by herself came running out white as a ghost. She said that someone touched her in there. I told her that it was used as an underground railway for freeing the slaves. Jason and Mark entered the barn by way of the ladder and they came out right away. They said that the anger in there was so bad that they didn't even want to deal with it right now. They said that they felt individuals who were in pain and were extremely angry. We all left the tunnel in a very big hurry.

"Is there anything we can do to help them?" I asked Jason. He said nothing short of an exorcism would help that room. They said the rest of the "barn" was clear. I wondered if we would find any more bodies buried in that room.

We all went upstairs and Shelly said that the living room was a hot bed of activity. Lots of entities moving about in that room. None were harmful she thought. After leaving the living room the team checked out the rest of the downstairs. They showed me on their monitor that there was activity in the kitchen but it was an good energy, nothing to be afraid in there. That it was a happy kitchen but that there was a little girl spirit still attached to this room. The library was not so happy, it had a heavy feeling in it Shelly said. She said that she could smell cigar smoke, the smell of dirt and smelly bodies, like body odor. She said that some old uniforms from the civil war which she examined for some family's had the same smell. So there had to have been military men in here at one time.

While going upstairs Tina let out a loud surprising gasp and had to grab the railing to keep from falling.

"Somebody just went through me going downstairs".

I had to bite my tongue to keep from saying anything about the house. Mark said that the portrait of Nathaniel was full of hate. Gee, I could have told him that one just by looking at the ugly thing.

As we went from room to room they reported not much activity until we came to the room overlooking the cemetery.

"Someone died in this room, I sense it was a woman. She was very sad and wanted to die" she stopped at that.

All the time that the team was doing their investigation Natasha was talking to them and interjecting things that she has felt. She had been told not to tell the team anything that had happened to her also.

When we came to the master bedroom Shelly and Tina both broke out in sweats. They said that this room has a very disturbing dark aura to it. Like Natasha they both said that the lady of the house still resides in this room. Jason and Mark had been taking notes, using their video cameras and watching their monitors while all of this was going on. Shelly felt as if someone was trying to choke her and she had to leave the room.

Tina and Natasha decided to see if they could together contact someone in the room. The vibrations in the room according to the monitor as soon as they started shot up. Tina felt a presence but said it was not a bad presence, she couldn't explain it, it was like that of a child but smaller, then it was gone. I suggested that we try again later after dark.

We went to the attic. As soon as I opened the door there was this blast of cold air that froze everybody to the bone. It was so cold we could see our breath.

Jason said "Oh, shit I don't like the feelings I'm getting. Dr. Thomas you had bettered speak to this house and do it soon or the activity is going to get worse".

Dr. Thomas led the way in. Shelly and Tina said at the same time "There is a presence in this room that doesn't want us in here".

All of the sudden this dark figure appeared right in front of Dr. Thomas. It looked like the man with the whip from my dream. It grabbed Dr. Thomas and throw him toward the door screaming "Get out".

I tried to be brave and shouted "No, this is my house now and you get out". With that I was thrown toward the door. Then boxes, crates, trunks and all sorts of things started being thrown at us. "Get out or die" it screamed. As we just barely made it through the door it slammed shut and we could hear things being thrown at the door still.

"Did you get that on film Mark?"

"Yeah, that was fantastic. I've never been through that before" he said out of breath.

"Who was that?" Tina asked.

"I'll bet that was Nathaniel himself. There must be something in that room that he is protecting and doesn't want anybody to find it. I wonder what it could be."

Dr. Thomas said scratching his chin. "I don't know."

I've been in there several times and nothing like that has ever happened. As a matter of fact I have gone through most of the stuff up there and didn't find anything out of the ordinary.

Here, you might want to read this. It's Angela's diary. It explains a lot of things" I said handing the doctor the diary.

I had forgotten, with all the excitement, that Dr. Jefferson was with us.

"Dr. Jefferson what do you think could be in the attic. You know a lot of the family history and such?" I asked.

"In all of my family records that I have read nothing was ever mentioned about the attic. So I haven't the slightest idea" he said setting a tray with cups and a large pot of coffee down on the coffee table.

"He could be dangerous. Not many spirits can make things move, they have to be very powerful to make things move the way he did. We need to go about this so that nobody gets hurt and remember Jonathan is in denial so we have to be cautious around him" Natasha said.

Tina said that later she would try to contact the spirits in the house to see if they would tell her what they want us to do or how we can help them.

"I would enjoy the challenge of speaking to the lady of the house, Angela is it? Although, any number of entities could pop up and try speaking to us so I'll have to direct my questions explicitly to her" she said as she started out of the room.

"Where are you going?" Dr. Thomas said.

"To the car, I need some of my equipment, I'll be right back" she called shutting the front door.

"You know Nathaniel was a very strong and powerful man when he was alive, I wonder if he could have carried all that hatred with him to the other side. He may be overpowering all the other spirits or entities here and not letting them cross over" I said questioningly to Dr. Thomas.

Jason piped up "Yeah, he might be so overpowering that he could take your head off, if you say the wrong thing".

Tina came back with an overnight bag setting it down. "Don't worry Jason, I know how to handle angry spirits".

"My dear, you have not come up against an entity that is as strong as this one. I really don't think we should try to speak to it until we have a little more knowledge about the things that went on in this house" Dr. Thomas said as he put on his reading glasses settling down in the chair next to the lamp.

I fixed sandwiches and more coffee for all of us. We gathered around the large dinning table and I took Dr. Thomas's cue and started telling everybody things that has happened since we moved in. Natasha and Dr. Jefferson chimed in also. I was amazed by the way the team took notes and asked direct questions about each room, the time of day, the weather and such about the happenings. When we were finished telling them everything, they asked that Dr. Jefferson, Natasha and I to leave the room so that they could plan their next move.

I made up the guest rooms in anticipation that the doctor and his team would want to stay the night to experience first hand any happenings. Dr. Jefferson stayed in one of the rooms. Natasha and I stayed in my room. Shelly and Tina shared a room. Jason and Mark each took one of the smaller rooms. After all were settled in we said good night and settled down waiting for the happenings to start, if any.

The house came alive right about midnight.

Shelly and Tina had been having a tough night, it started out by being woken up by a horrible, hideous and pungent odor in the room. They couldn't find the source of the order so when they attempted to open the windows and/or the door to let the order out, neither the windows nor the door would open no matter how hard they tried. As quickly as the order started it stopped then apparitions started sitting on their beds, shaking the beds violently and even disappearing in to the closet. When they opened the door to the closet to see what was in there, there was nothing just clothes.

Jason who was sleeping in one of the small rooms had been

fascinated by watching the rocking chair in his room levitating and rocking in mid air, turning upside down and crashing to the floor. He has one of his monitors on and it registered very high with electric vibrations. He tried to take pictures but his camera was snatched from his hands and thrown on the bed.

The doctors had been experiencing the smell of cigar smoke in their room. It was so bad that they had to open the window to let the smoke out.

Before we Natasha and I went into my room for the night she informed me that the lady of the house is very disturbed tonight and she felt like something was going to happen. We had trouble keeping the covers on the bed, every time we pulled the covers up, something would pulled them off onto the floor. Then we would hear giggles. Natasha was levitated off the bed, turned on her head and dropped. I got mad and told the entity to quit it or else and instantly got kicked in the leg.

What really got to everybody was the horrible screams emitting from Mark's room. We all met in the hallway. Dr Thomas and Dr. Jefferson and tried to open the door to his room, but no matter what they did it wouldn't open. Just as sudden as it started the screams stopped and Mark's door creaked open.

As we entered the room we found Mark huddled in terror in a dark corner of his room. We tried the light switch but the lights would not turn on. As we approached Mark we all got chills crawling up our bodies. It was so cold in the room that everybody could see their breath. Shelly said that something was in the room with us. Just then a see through apparition appeared, it was sort of smokey and emitted a eerie glow which illuminated the room. Dr. Thomas attempted to touch it and it disappeared.

While we were still in his room, we heard very loud footsteps on the ceiling above our head, it was so loud that we had to cover our ears. The started out just walking then they took off running down the hall for a minute or so and then just stopped. We heard breaking glass and then all got quite. Dr. Jefferson asked what was on the next floor and I told him it was two large rooms where the slaves that worked in the house used to live.

"I'll check it out to see if anything is broken up there and I'll be right back" he said as he started toward the stairs.

"Don't go alone, doctor" Shelly said.

"I'll go with you doc" Jason said leading the way.

After checking everything they could think of that might be broken, they returned and said they couldn't find anything.

Nobody got much sleep the rest of the night. Jonathan would be home in a couple of days so if we were going to attempt something we had better do it in the morning or tomorrow night at the latest.

We all started the day off with a big breakfast. This morning I made the coffee extra strong. Everybody felt like they had hangovers. Tina opted out of breakfast, said that she always fasted before performing a seance, which he said she was going to do tonight.

This house, this horrible house, I pray that Dr. Thomas and his team can clear this house so our, or maybe I should say my life, could get back to normal. I am so tired of living with undesirable entities, having the feeling that my energy is being drained out of my body and being suddenly woken up at night by something that isn't there, that I could just scream.

I have decided that no matter what Jonathan says I'm going to clear this house if it's the last thing I do, short of burning it down.

Shelly spent most of the day preparing the formal dinning room and herself for the seance tonight. She said that if we can contact one of the entities and find out why they are still here, then maybe we can clear the house.

The doctors, Mark and Jason prepared the tape records, and video equipment to record the seance. I couldn't help but wonder if that would work or if it was going to stir up more trouble.

I knew I would be in the way, I went outside for a while.

Natasha joined me after a while and was fascinated by the headstones we encountered as we walked among the graves in the cemetery. She said that we should talk to the spirts and let them know what was going to happen tonight and ask them to participate with us. As she passed by each grave she laid her hands on them and asked them to please communicate with us tonight to let us know if there is something that was unfinished by them before they died we could help them finish it.

She was it was strange that when we got close to Nathaniel's tomb said she didn't feel anything. She said that it was as if his spirit was not there. She said that when she got close to Angela's grave there was a heavy feeling, an almost suffocating feeling, there. It was like something evil was preventing any good vibrations to come from it. We looked for the graves of the baby which Constance had and as I figured it wasn't there. Could the bones of the baby we found be Constance's baby?

"Let's try to communicate with Nathaniel to see what he did with Constance's baby. Ask him if the bones we found are the child's bones. If they are I want to give them a proper burial" I said to Natasha.

"I don't think it would be a good idea to communicate with him. He may be the evil force at work here and that may bring up more anger and things might get out of hand" she replied, knowing more about these things than I did.

During the evening Shelly instructed all of us on what to do before and during the seance. When dinner was served she told us that we shouldn't have any alcohol because she wanted us to have clear heads about us. The witching hour was midnight. Tina said that the moon would be the fullest then and since it was All Hallows Eve, Halloween, the spirits would be more than willing to participate.

As midnight approached Tina covered the dinning table with a white table cloth and had set out 3 taper candles in crystal holders. The smell of Frankensence and Sandalwood incense was in the air, she said together they were for grounding and protection.

There were so much equipment in the room it looked like a movie set. Tape recorders and video cameras were set up to record what happened here tonight, if anything.

There were a tablet and several pens next to where Tina was going to set. That was to be used for automatic writing if need be.

About 11:30 p.m. Shelly had all of us come into the dining room. There was soft mellow music playing and the lights were dim. A different kind of incense was burning, this time I couldn't quite make it out, but it had a very relaxing effect on me. I'll have to ask her what it is so that I can get some for me.

As we took our seats, Shelly started.

"I want to start off by telling you that the more relaxed you are with this the better of you will be. So for a little while just sit in here, nobody talking, just listen to the music and breath in the incense and try to relax".

By the time we really got down to business I was really relaxed. Could it have been the particular incense Shelly was using? I hadn't notice but a half hour had passed and it was midnight. The grandfather clock in the hall was chiming the time.

Shelly continued, "This night the moon is full and we are here to try communicate with any spiritual entity that would like to let us know they are here".

Tina turned off the lights, the music and lit the three candles. If the night wasn't eerie enough we had to sit in the dark with only candles. This is something we never did back in the city.

"I'm going to try to communicate with the entities that are in this house. Join hands, at all times during the seance keep holding hands. Try not to break the circle unless the entities become overly aggressive, then and only then break the circle and turn on the lights. Spirits in this house we ask that you communicate with us and move among us. Welcome to the spirits of air, fire, water and earth. I summon, stir and call ye up mighty ones of the north, south, east and west. Portals which allow us to communicate with the spirits in this house. Hail and welcome. Spirits that live in this house I call to you to show us a sign if you are with us".

Shelly repeated this several times with nothing happening.

"Spirits that live in this house, if you are here I welcome you to use my body as a portal to communicate with us".

She just barely got this out before this misty vale of light, a ungodly blue glow, came over her and her facial features seemed to change and the room got suddenly very cold.

"I have told you, you are not welcome in this house" came a female the voice from Shelly.

"I have to tell you that you are in danger" it continued.

I asked "Who are you?" Who are we in danger from?"

"Beware of the one who walks in anger" came response.

"Who is it?" I asked.

All of the sudden the wind kicked up swirling everything in the room and a ungodly scream that would curdle already curdled milk echoed in the room. I felt like someone was strangling me. I couldn't breath but I didn't break the circle even though I really wanted to try to move the "hands" from around my neck.

"You're in danger doctor" came the voice as Shelly pointed toward Dr. Jefferson.

Dr. Jefferson looked at her with a shocked questioning look. Someone or something took over Tina's body and called to the entity that was choking me.

"Let her go!"

This time it was a very distinctive male voice speaking.

"She has nothing to do with what happened here. Let her go!" the voice boomed again. The hands released me. Things were thrown around the room, the wind got very violent and then the doors to the dinning room slammed shut.

Just as quickly as the doors shut they flew open again. Dr. Jefferson was thrown against the wall by invisible hands. He was picked up again and thrown against the opposite was from the table this time he crumpled to the floor. The circle had been broken and everything stopped. Someone had turned on the lights.

Shelly collapsed face down on the table. We all jumped up to check on her and Dr. Jefferson. He was ok he said. The room was warm again. She slowly lifted her head, "Did you get that on tape?" was all she said before she fainted.

The guys carried her to the living room and laid her on the couch. Dr. Thomas checked her vitals and said that they were ok. When she came to he handed her a glass of Brandy.

"I have never experienced two entities entering my body before in all the times I have been doing seances. The first was not a very strong entity but the second on was such a strong entity. He seemed to be in control of everything. I wish I had his strength" she said sitting up weakly.

"Did you get any feeling as to whom it might have been?" Dr. Thomas asked.

"No, I know that the one entity that first took over was afraid. I'm going to check the video tape to see what happened and see if I can determine anything from that, the second was definitely a male but I got the feeling that he was definitely not the entity that we encountered in the attic the other night", she said as she got up and headed back into the dinning room.

Tina, Mark, Jason, Dr. Thomas and Dr. Jefferson all went into the dinning room following after her to check out things. I told Natasha that I had had enough for the night and all I wanted to do was get a glass of wine, got outside get some fresh air and "relax".

When we got outside Natasha asked "How's your neck? Let me check to see if there are any marks."

Surprisingly my neck didn't hurt and there weren't any marks, it was like nothing happened.

"Man, I tell you if we don't get those entities or spirits out of this house soon I'm going to go bonkers".

"I have faith in the team. They seem to know what they are doing and maybe they will be able to tell you what can be done before Jonathan gets back home tomorrow".

I had forgotten about Jonathan with everything that has been going on.

"Natasha what I'm I going to do? He will be furious if he finds out what happened here tonight. How am I going to explain it to him?"

"Slow down, let's go in and tell the team your concerns and maybe they can think of something."

We didn't notice the glow coming from the cemetery moving toward the house as we went inside the house.

"Jonathan will be home tomorrow! What are we going to do?" I almost yelled when I burst into the dining room. They all look at me with surprise. Dr. Jefferson, took my by the arm and led me out of the room.

"They are working on a plan to exorcize the entities out of the house. We know that Jonathan will be home tomorrow and they have a plan for that to. Now, why don't you and Natasha go into the kitchen and make us a strong pot of coffee and when it is ready bring it in and we will go over everything with you. Ok, that's my girls" he said in an almost patronizing tone.

Dumbfounded I turned and walked into the kitchen and obeyed by making a pot of coffee.

"Hey, wait a minute, who does he think he is?" I said when I finally snapped to.

"Calm down, he was just making sure that we weren't too excited when we heard what they had to say and that way we could except it better".

Right then all of the lights in the house went out and it got very cold. As my eyes adjusted to the light I noticed that there was this glowing light coming from outside. Everybody had rushed into the living room.

"Dr. Jefferson what do you think that is?" I asked. I hadn't noticed but I was holding onto his arm. He looked at me and raised his eyebrow. I let go and gave him a half ass smile.

He walked closer to the window and said "I don't know, it seems to be all around the house".

"It's the spirits from the cemetery. They are all wanting to tell us something but there are so many voices I can't understand them" Tina said covering her ears. Here me all spirits trying to communicate with us. Here me. I can't understand you if you all talk at one time. I know your time is short but please communicate one at a time" Tina yelled.

Mark had gotten a note pad and Tina was frantically writing. Shelly was speaking softly into a tape recorder. The doctors and the boy were frantically taking pictures and moving around the inside of the house with video cameras to see if they could catch anything on tape. After what seemed to be a half hour, the lights came back on and the glow was gone. Tina exhausted set the pen down.

"Let's see what we have here" as Dr. Thomas took the note pad and sat down trying to make out what was written.

"Get out, someone is going to die, bury the bones, Constance, leave now, search attic, trunk, Angela angry, release spirt, Nathaniel's wrath, look behind wall. I think that someone was trying to tell us something about the attic" he said with a puzzled questioning look on his face.

"The other night when we were forced out of the attic by that entity, could we have been too close to whatever it is that the spirts doesn't want us to find?" I asked.

"I don't know but the attic does deserve another look" he said.

"Jonathan will be home in the morning" as I looked at the clock which was chiming 3 a.m. "He will be home in less than 6 hours" I said. "We should get up into that attic right now and start looking. If all of us check the trunks and bang on the walls maybe we will find what ever it is that the spirts was trying to prevent us from finding" I said starting out of the room.

"Wait a minute. The spirits also said someone is going to die".

That stopped me in my tracks. "What do you think it means? Spirits can't hurt people, can they?" I asked.

"You saw how it tossed us out of the room didn't you? Didn't you see how they slammed Dr. Jefferson against the wall in the dinning room? How about you being strangled? It could have just as easily tossed something through one of us to kill us. Spirts can be gentle or as we have seen they can be violent. We can't just go barging in there. It would be waiting for us. It could have been one of the spirits communicating to us just now."

"Ok, now what do we do?"

I saw headlights coming up the drive way. Who could that be at this hour? In my worst fears I feared that it might be Jonathan and he wouldn't appreciate everybody here at this hour. So I asked everybody to get out of sight until I found out who it was. My worst fears come true as Jonathan's car drove up to the front door.

"Everybody out the back door, it's Jonathan" I called quietly. I ran upstairs, stripping on the way, grabbed my nightgown and rumpled the bed to make it look like I had been sleeping, and climbed into bed.

I heard the front door creaking open and closed, then his footsteps on the stairs. I had to try to calm my breathing down and make it look convincing when he came in. He went right by the bed and into the bathroom, showered and then came to bed. Climbing into bed he reached over me and held me tight.

"Hey, what you breathing so hard for? Are you that glad I'm home" he breathed in my ears.

"Yes darling" I replied rolling over and reciprocating the affection.

Afterwards, I quietly said, "You're home early, how did your meeting go".

Yawning Jonathan said "I missed you. Meeting went ok, I tell you about in the morning" and he drifted off to sleep. I laid awake for a while wondering if everybody had gotten away ok. Must have because Jonathan didn't say anything about hearing anything. I hope he didn't hear anything.

After breakfast Jonathan kept watching the clock and then surprised me by saying that he had been talking to a friend on his trip that knew all about ghosts and stuff like that and he thought that maybe I would like meeting him. We could discuss the "happenings" here at the house. Well, you know what I have been going through and now he tells me this. I didn't know whether to be mad at him, hit him or hug him.

Natasha had been listening to our conversation and almost said something about we had already had someone here, but after me giving her a quick don't say anything look, we just decided to hear Jonathan out. He explained that this friend of his had a Ph.D. in parapsychology and had been "ghost busting" for several years and was quite good at it. After he had heard what Jonathan had to say he said that he wanted to come here and meet me and see the house for himself.

"When is he coming?" I asked. Right then there was a knock on the front door.

"Now" Jonathan said almost running to the front door. I looked over at Natasha questioningly and she shrugged her shoulders.

Amy, Natasha, please meet Dr. Vince Castle".

Jonathan introduced his rather nice looking young man. I'd say he was in his early thirties, blonde hair, the deepest bluest eyes I'd ever seen and that smile, it could stop a bus. He didn't look anything like a ghost buster would look like, not like the ones on TV, anyway. He was drop dead gorgeous. I could see that Natasha was quite taken with him and was at the point of drooling all over, so I quickly said "Welcome to our haunted house". With that we all laughed.

"I was looking around outside before I came in and you know that his place has many spirits that reside here? As a matter of fact, there was one that was sitting on the front porch swing when I walked up. We had a pleasant conversation" he said quite seriously. Seeing the surprised look on my face he added "Just joking. There wasn't anybody there, but here are many spirits that do live here".

"You're probably wondering why a guy like me is in this type of line. Well, when I was younger, I had one of those "near death experiences" and since then I see ghosts, when I don't see them I can sense them, I know when one come close. As a matter of fact, I sense several are in this room right now listening to what I am telling you. We all looked around to see if we could see anything. They sometimes talk to me but mostly they give me a sign or lead me to something that they need taken care of so they can cross over". He got this strange look on his face, cocked his head to the right, arched his right eyebrow and shook his head like he was listening to someone.

"Just kidding" he smiled.

Let's take him out to the stone circle to see if he can sense anything there" Natasha interjected, breaking the moment, as she caressed his strong arm. "It's kind of like Stone Hedge. You would like the walk across the field, through the grove of trees and the to this circle. It is such a nice day, what do you say?" She said looking up at him with longing in her eyes.

"Let him get settled in and then you two can walk over there if you want to, I need to talk to Jonathan and get him caught up on things around here" I said patting Jonathan on the butt.

With that Jonathan showed Vince to his room, Natasha stayed to help.

Jonathan and I went to the kitchen to let them settle in. He turned to me and said "Ok, what have you been up to since I have been gone?"

"Well" I started not really knowing if I should tell him everything or just a little so I said "I'll make a long story short. It is like this. After you left Dr. Jefferson came over with a friend of his Dr. Thomas, you met him at the barbeque, remember. He is the head of a paranormal psychology group. Dr. Jefferson told Dr. Thomas what I had told him and Dr. Thomas brought his team, they were at the barbeque also, to investigate the house and the land. They all had different types of powers, psychic, medium and the like, so they toured the outside of the house, part of the barn and the house. Each making notes on things they found. We all stared one night to go into the attic and this figure appeared before us, yelling, and whipping this huge whip.

"A whip?" Jonathan exclaimed.

"Yeah, a whip. It through us out of the attic. After that the tem decided that we needed a seance. So with cameras and tape recorders we held a seance on Halloween night and boy that was exciting. First of all Shelly was taken over by one spirit then another. I was being choked and one spirit told the spirit choking me to stop it. Then Dr. Jefferson was thrown against the wall. The door slammed shut, the lights went on and off. It was wild. They are supposed to show me the tapes but I haven't gotten to see them yet".

All the time I was telling Jonathan this I didn't notice it but Vince and Natasha were standing in the doorway.

"Sounds like this spirit doesn't like someone here very much. I'd like to meet these people and see the tape also. That is if Jonathan doesn't mind". Vince said scratching his chin.

"You two go for a walk and I'll call Dr. Jefferson and make arrangements for us to go over to his house".

"Hi doc, had Dr. Thomas's team been able to get anything from the videos and/or the pictures?" I asked excitedly.

He said "You won't believe your eyes when you see what I have seen. I had a hard time grasping it. You need to see this as soon as possible. Do you need to make an excuse to Jonathan to come over or do we need to wait until he goes on a trip again?"

"No, Jonathan has a friend that talked to him about the things that are going on here and is actually really excited to see the video. He brought his friend home with him. He is kind of a ghost buster and he want to come along with us, if that is ok with you?"

"Sure, as a matter of fact, why don't we make it sort of a barbeque ghost busting type afternoon?"

"Sound great we'll see you around one." I said hanging up the phone and turning to Jonathan. I hadn't notice that Vince and Natasha had left the house, but Jonathan did.

"Well, what did he say?" Jonathan as me.

"He said that we won't believe what they have come up with and that we are going to make it sort of a barbeque ghost busting type afternoon, so put on your levis and help me make some potato salad to take with us."

Jonathan slipped his arms around my waist as I started to pull out a large pot for the potatoes.

"Hey, lady what's the rush, I have been gone a long time and I haven't been able to really get you alone for five minutes. I'm sure Nat will keep Vince out for a while. Let's take some time for ourselves, shall we?" he said as he started kissing the nape of my neck and rubbing my breasts.

"That sire will get you a good ten minutes, if you are a really good boy" I said in my sexiest voice and batting my eyes. Pulling away I took both of his hands and led him toward the stairs.

Chapter 8

Natasha and Vince had just walked into the clearing where the stone circle was when Vince said that he have a very bad feeling about this place. Natasha had explained to him on their walk over that she was a psychic and that maybe together they could sense something and get a vision about the place.

Vince walked around a little noticing that there were smaller stones a few yard away from the stone circle. He waked over to them, he instantly felt that this was once a place of great sorrow.

He got a vision that there was something under the stones like a chamber or something and started looking for an entrance. Natasha saw what he was doing and started looking also but she didn't know what she was looking for.

"What are we looking for?"

"See if you can find a lever or something. I get the feeling that I have to go under ground to find something"

He came to this one particular looking stone that looked

like a handle. When he touched it he saw a vision of stairs with torches lit going down under the alter.

"Here goes nothing" he said as he turned the handle and the large alter stone slid to one side.

Natasha gave out a cry of surprise as she was sitting on the stone. Jumping off as it moved she couldn't believe her eyes. They both stood there looking from each other to the opening in the ground.

Vince started down, Natasha grabbed his arm.

"Wait a minute, were not going down there.

"Stay here if you want, but I'm going down to see what is there."

"Maybe we should go back to the house and get a flash light or something."

"I have a lighter and I'll light a torch. I saw them in my vision going all the way to the bottom. Come on, it will be fun" He said disappearing in the darkness.

Giving out a sign of exasperation, Natasha followed him down the steps.

The air was musty but it had a pleasant sweet smell. As they descended down the steps Vince grabbed two torches and lit them, handing one to Natasha. They were surprised by the size of the room they had just stepped into. The symbols on the walls looked Inca or Aztec. There were dust covered relics on the ground, they were animal shapes of all different sizes.

"Vince, I don't like this place. I have seen some of these symbols and they look like they are Voodoo symbols."

"Nat they are Inca or Aztec"

Vince, I have studied Voodoo practices and these are definitely Voodoo symbols and I'll be this is a place of either worship or they performed some kind of rituals here. Let's get out now!"

"I am going to look around, if you feel uncomfortable go back up" Vince said sharply.

The room was huge. It has a large stone pedestal at the

end of the room and a large stone chair, like a throne. It was carved with lots of symbols. When Vince placed his hand on the chair he saw images of people dressed in long robes, feather headdresses, their faces painted and one man in particular had on this very large golden chest plate.

Not wanting to be left out Natasha felt the throne and had a vision of someone lying on the alter crying for help.

"Wow, that was intense, I have never had a vision so real before. Do you get them also?"

"Yeah, I get them all the time. You stay here and let me walk around a little before we try that again, ok?" He said kissing her on the forehead.

As he walked around he experienced visions of people being ritually executed, sacrificed. There was the sound of drums beating and people dancing to the sound of the drums. The strongest place in the circle was the altar. He saw blood everywhere. There was this one entity that he kept seeing always hold this double edged dagger with blood dripping from it. It was chanting something but he couldn't make it out.

Vince decided that maybe if he and Natasha together placed their hands on the altar that maybe they could see the visions more clearly. They knelt down before the altar and held hands, placing their free hands on the altar.

Instantly, Natasha was thrown away from the alter and onto the ground. Vince grabbed her asking her is she was alright.

"Someone or something grabbed me by my hair and yanked me away from the altar" she said rubbing the back of her head.

"Maybe this isn't such a good idea".

"Let's try something different. How about I set on the altar and you place your hands on the altar to see what happens".

"Ok, but if I get thrown again, I am going back to the house and you can do this by yourself" Natasha said still rubbing her head.

Vince climbed on the altar but before he sat down, he stretched out his arms above his head and calling to the gods he prayed that they protect he and Natasha in their task. He sat down slowly anticipating that he may be thrown off. Nothing happened. He closed he eyes and started telling Natasha the things he was seeing.

"Things are flashing by me really fast but there is a lot of sacrificing and blood shed. There are people who are just standing there staring like there were zombies or something."

"Wait, there is a figure coming up the walkway to your left. No, don't turn around, let the figure get closer. I want to see who it is. My God, she is dressed like a Voodoo priestess. She looks like Amy. She is holding this very long curved dagger, like I saw before. She looks like she is in some sort of trance. Man what a body".

Natasha almost hit him but figured she would wait and do that later when they were on their way home.

"She is speaking a language I don't quite understand, but from the looks of things she means business."

Looking down he sees a child lying on the stone. He is crying and holding his stomach. Man, Vince thinks this is getting real bazar.

"Natasha put your hands on the altar very slowly."

She did as she was told and all of the sudden she was in the middle of the ceremony. She was dressed in a gown like the priestess and wore a smaller head dress similar to that of the priestess. The priestess figure handed her a bowl with what looked like blood in it. Natasha looked around to see if she could see Vince. She could vaguely make out his ghost like appearance sitting on the altar. She was afraid to say anything for fear that she would get stabbed with that ugly dagger held by the priestess.

Vince whispered to her "Don't worry if it gets too weird, I'll get us out".

There were men dressed in head dressed but much, much smaller dancing and chanting all around the two women. The male child on the altar was crying and Natasha understood him to say "Please, no". She wanted to stop. Vince sensing that she wanted to stop whispered to her to give it one more minute then they will pull out.

The priestess figure dipped her fingers into the blood and smeared it on the child in a strange but familiar pattern. It was a blessing of some kind. Th e woman then took the dagger and instead of stabbing the child cut a small circle inside the symbol and placing her hand inside the circle pulled out a black looking substance and the child cried out in pain. The woman place the substance in the altar fire and chanted very loudly. Natasha understood it to be a healing chant. This woman must be a medical shaman because when the fire died down the child stopped crying and said the pain was gone.

Natasha said "Thank God."

The priestess looked at her wide eyed as if Natasha had cursed to the gods or something.

Vince knew that they were in trouble and stood up, calling to Natasha to take her hands off the altar. He climbed off the altar as fast as he could and noticed that Natasha was still kneeling before the altar with her hands still on it. He reach down to her to help her remove her hands and some unseen force threw him against one of the stones knocking him out cold.

Natasha started moving backwards as the men started toward her. She wondered why Vince hadn't helped her stop this. As she looked around she saw him laying crumpled on the ground next to a stone.

"Vince, help me" she screamed.

The men were on her, grabbing at her, tearing at her clothes, she could feel the flesh on her arms and legs being scratched.

"Help me" she screamed again.

She knew she had to get to him and try to wake him up. Defending herself the best way she could she finally made her way over to Vince. She kicked at him and he moved slightly. She kicked again this time really hard on his butt.

"Wake up, help me get out of this!" She yelled.

The men stopped, looking at her wondering what it was she was saying but then started right back attacking her.

Just then everything went black.

When she opened her eyes she found herself lying in the

grass by the stream with Vince bending over her. He had carried her there and was doctoring her scratches the best way he could.

"My God, what happened? That was not supposed to happen, was it? How did I get to be a physical presence in something that took place ages ago?" she asked, trying to move but couldn't because she hurt too bad.

"I don't know how any of that happened. Did you see that priestess? It looked like Amy" Vince replied, not really knowing how to answer her questions.

"Why was I attacked? Was it something I said? How did they physically attack me and scratch me? Would I have been killed it they succeeded in getting me to the altar? How did I know what they were saying?" Natasha asked looking back at the stone circle clearing.

"I've never had an experience like that before when someone was physically involved. I am going to have to get in contact with my professor friend at the college and ask him about this. This may be worth exploring more" he said excitedly walking back and forth scratching his chin.

"Not with me you don't mister!" Natasha said getting up.

"But Nat we could open up a new field of research together."

"No! I'm going back to the house. Are you coming or should I leave you to your voodoo buddies and the priestess with the body?"

"Ok, but let's talk about this when we get back to house and write down exactly what happened that way I can do a paper for the college".

"Oh, so that's what this is all about. A paper for the college. Count me out buddy. Are you here to check out Jonathan and Amy's house just to write a paper too? Oh, yeah I forgot something" she said hitting him hard on the arm walking away.

"Hey, what was that for? Wait for me" he asked rubbing his arm.

Chapter 9

"Jonathan, do you think Dr. Jefferson, Dr. Thomas and your friend will be able to find out what is going on here and take care of it for us?"

Sleepily he yawned, stretched and wrapped his arms around me, "Maybe baby, I hope whatever it is that they do it quickly so we can get down to some serious living here" he said kissing the back of my neck.

"Amy, Amy where are you?" I heard Natasha calling from downstairs.

"Amy, Jonathan were are you? I need you" Natasha cried.

"Something's wrong" I said jumping out of bed, leaving Jonathan in a heap. Grabbing my robe I rushed down stairs.

"Natasha, what's wrong."

I heard water running in the kitchen and headed that way. I was horrified when I found Natasha, she looked like she had been beat up, she was shaking so that she almost dropped the glass she was holding.

"What did he do to you? Get her some Brandy" I said grabbing a chair for her to sit down.

"He didn't do anything to me, it was the stone circle" she said as she began to cry.

"The stone circle?" Jonathan said as he walking into the kitchen. "What happened there. Oh great, first it is the house and now the stone circle. What next the barn will become twisted also?"

As she explained what happened but before she could tell up about the "paper" part, Vince came walking into the kitchen. She looked at him as if she could throw daggers at him. I have never seen her so upset or angry at anybody like that before.

"We combined our abilities and she, unfortunately, was the portal which allowed what she experienced come through. She has great abilities. I tried to tell her that but she got mad at me and punched my arm. What was that for anyway? Did you tell Amy that the priestess looked a lot like her?"

"What? A priestess that looked like me. What are you talking about? You had better start telling me everything before I really get upset and as you to leave."

He went into great depth about the ceremony they experienced and the fact that the high priestess could possibly come up form the underground and cause havoc here, but he didn't know for sure. He really would need to do more research, but Natasha was not willing to go through that again, so we may never know for sure.

"Could that entity have hurt Natasha seriously?"

Jonathan listened intently to all that was said, then interjected "Let's just take care of the house for now. The stone circle can wait".

Natasha looked at him "Thank you and Amen to that. I'm going upstairs and take a long hot bath. Amy, do you have any antiseptic I can put on these scratches?"

We walked out of the room together. The men just stood there looking at us as we walked away.

"Why did you go there?" Isn't it bad enough we have this problem or what Amy calls it a haunting here at the house?"

"Jon, I didn't know where we were going and I surely didn't expect anything like that to happen. I figured it was just some stone circle that some theoretical group put there for outdoor plays or something like that."

"Well we had bettered get the girls over to Dr. Jefferson's house before they both move out and leave us."

When we all got to Dr. Jefferson's house the smell of the barbeque made me remember that I hadn't eaten all day, so when Dr. Jefferson suggested that we eat first and relax before we saw what Dr. Thomas and his team had I was grateful.

Jonathan introduced Vince to everybody. The team and Dr. Thomas swarmed all around him asking him all sorts of questions. I could hear him telling them about what happened at the stone circle and looking over at Natasha.

She was in no mood to talk to anybody about anything and told them so in no uncertain words without being rude. She mentioned to me before we left the house that she thought she had stayed long enough and that she wanted to go back to the city. She wanted to leave that ghost busting bum and the stone circle behind her. She told me that what we need to do is burn the house down, sow the grounds with salt, move the bodies from the cemetery to a decent cemetery and move back to the city. I figured I would let her cool off and then maybe try to entice her to stay a little longer later.

The afternoon was just right, not too hot and there was a nice cool gentle breeze blowing. Nora buzzed around us like a mother hen, making sure that we all had plenty of food and drinks. She was so happy to have such a large gathering, said that it had been too long since Dr. Jefferson had entertained and that she should do it more often. Dr. Jefferson looked over at me when she wasn't looking and rolled his eyes like oh brother here we go again.

As early evening came and everybody had their fill of food

and drink, Dr. Thomas suggested that we all go into the house and he would show us what they had.

I was completely shocked at what I was looking at. At first there was only a mist above Shelly's head but then it started assuming a form, it was the form of a woman. We couldn't make out who it was. The camera positioned over to me showed this mist of a woman hovering over me. Its features were a little bit more distinctive and we could make out that it was Constance, or what looked like Constance choking me. When the male voice came from Shelly the camera over her showed what looked like Zachary's appearance in Shelly's face. The camera over Dr. Jefferson showed this very dark shape hovering all around him and picking him up and slamming him into the wall. Then it disappeared through the doors, just to reappear, pick up Dr. Jefferson again and throw him across the room. Then disappear completely. The camera over Tina showed several entities reaching their hands out to us. Then they were gone.

"Well, we know that Zachary and Constance are still here. Why was she choking Amy. Who that dark entity was I would have to assume it was Nathaniel due to the violent way he treated Dr. Jefferson" Dr. Thomas stated looking a bit confused.

"Why would Constance want to hurt me? I haven't done anything. As a matter of fact I'm not related to any of them in the first place". I stated very loud thinking that I could make the entities understand.

"Constance knows that you are not the one because when Zachary told her that you were not involved she let go, didn't she?"

I nodded.

"Well, I think that Tina and Shelly should try to communicate individually with Zachary to see if they can get him to let them know what he wants, so maybe they can help him cross over." Dr. Jefferson said looking over at Shelly and Tina.

"If I can get him to tell me what unfinished business he has, then maybe he can help me understand why he hasn't crossed over. Maybe he is still trying to find Topieta. If you know anything about her and what happened to her that will help me when and if I can communicate with him" Tina said looking at me and Jonathan.

"I understand that maybe Dr. Jefferson would know more about what happened to her for his family kept very good historical records". I said looking at Dr. Jefferson, who shook his head indicated yes.

Nora came in bringing refreshments and snacks. "Doctor, there was a telephone message for you from the university about those bones you took to them a while back. They said that they wanted to go to Mr. Jonathan's house to see if they can find anymore. I told them that they would have to talk to you and Mr. Jonathan about that".

"Oh great, more people snooping around the house" Jonathan said in disgust.

"Sounds like we don't have much time to get things done around here before more people starting investigating. Guys I think that we should go to the Chamberlain house tonight and get started. Dr. Jefferson can you get the information to us now?" Dr. Thomas said.

As Dr. Jefferson left the room Mark said he still has some great still pictures of what was going on if anybody is interested.

When Dr. Jefferson came back he handed the journals and diaries to everybody. Tina was reading one of the diaries, she commented to Dr. Jefferson how well they kept them, but she wondered how they knew what happened to whom and when. Dr. Jefferson explained that his great grandfather was Angela's lover and he was the one who wrote most of the entries in the books.

"Maybe it's your great grandfather that is the one who is menacing Amy and Jonathan and doesn't understand that he is dead also. Do you know how he died?" Tina asked.

"I'm not sure, but I could do some checking in the local historian association to see if they have any information. If they don't I'll try to look him up on computer. Maybe there is some burial record I can find on him". He started to leave but Tina grabbed his arm.

"Here use my computer, that way it will get us started faster", she said handing him her laptop.

He was startled at first but took it, sat down and started typing. After a few minutes he looked up and said "I found him. He is buried not far from here. I'll go to the county seat to see if I can get a copy of his death certificate. That will tell us what he died from, I hope and when he died" he said as he was heading for the front door. "I'll be back as soon as possible" we heard as the door slammed shut.

While he was gone we all went back to our house, might as well return to the "scene of the crime" so to speak. For some reason I remembered the dream I had about the lady in the attic pointing at one of the trunks and the doll I threw. I left the group downstairs and ventured up to the attic. I had to find that trunk.

When I opened the door the smell was rancid. I had never smelled that before when I was up here. I quickly opened the two small windows to get some air in here. I moved box after box looking for the trunk, finally finding it in a corner of the attic which I hadn't gotten to yet in my explorations before. The trunk was more of a very, very large steamer chest like the ones you would see used on like the Titanic or something like that. It was too heavy for me to move. While standing there wondering what to do I was scared by a voice behind me.

"Hey" came the voice as I let out a small scream and wheeling around to see Mark standing just inside the attic door.

"What's ya doing?" he asked.

"I have to move this trunk so I can look inside it. Come help me".

The trunk was very heavy and Mark and I struggled to move it. I called downstairs for Jonathan to come help and upon hearing foot steps on the stairs I went back into the attic. I was focused on trying to get the lock open and I didn't look to see who had come in the door until it slammed shut with such force that it rattled the windows.

The dark shadow from the seance was hovering at the door.

"Get out!" it boomed. "Get out. Get out" the voice continued with such volume that it hurt our ears.

Defiantly I screamed back "No. This is my house now and I am not going anywhere."

With that all hell broke loose. The wind started whirling everything around the room, Mark and I had to duck to keep from being hit by flying boxes and things. Mark was lifted up as if he was going to be broken in half and thrown across the room slamming into a very large trunk. He fell to the floor in a heap.

"Get out of here, you are not wanted here and I am not going to give up on getting you out of my house" I tried screaming above all the noise.

I felt this horrific pain and all went black.

When I woke up the room was still and the dark shape was gone. I started to get up but the pain in my head and back was so intense that I laid back.

"Mark, Mark, are you alright" no response.

I forced myself to get up and crawl over to where Mark was. He was bleeding from the side of his face, he was out cold. I figured I had bettered get help. Crawling was the best I could do for now, so across the room I crawled to get to the door and scream for help.

I sat there and watched to make sure that this time when the footsteps on the stairs were heard it was Jonathan and everybody else coming toward the attic.

"What happened" Jonathan said helping me up.

"I'll tell you later, help Mark" I said pointing at him.

"I think he has a concussion. Help me get him downstairs so I can examine him" said Dr. Thomas.

After making sure that Mark was going to be alright, I explained to everybody what had happened and why I was in the attic.

"Since the entities are getting more and more violent, let's not go wondering off by ourselves any more, agreed?" Jonathan questioned looking at everybody. Everybody shook their head in agreement.

"What was so dammed important in that stupid trunk that you just had to get anyway? If it was just some more stupid piece of junk to put around the house I'm going to be pissed" Jonathan said glaring at me.

"Hear me out before you go jumping to conclusions, ok? I had a dream wherein this entity of a lady was pointing to that trunk. Then in that same dream there was a doll in the attic that when the dark shadow came yielding his whip at me I through the doll at it and it screamed and vanished. Then tonight when Mark and I tried to get the trunk open the dark shadow showed up again and wouldn't let us open the trunk. So there has to be something in that trunk or about that trunk and/or the doll that the dark shadow doesn't want us to see or know about. "

"Ok, when Dr. Jefferson gets back the guys will go back to the attic and get that stupid trunk out of there and bring it downstairs to open it" Dr. Thomas intervened.

"In the meantime how about taking care of Mark and staying out of trouble" Jonathan said sort of scolding me.

Shelly, Tina and Natasha had been all in the dining room with the door closed while all of this was taking place. The doors opened and out they all came, looking very worn out.

"What in the devil were you three doing in there?" Dr. Thomas asked.

"Well, we decided together we would combine out powers and try to speak to the lady of the house. She didn't show up but the one they call Constance did. She said that she was looking for her baby and needed out help to find it. Then we tried contacting Zachary but somebody by the name of Jacob popped in. He said that his father was the one that didn't want us to see what was in the attic. He told us that we have to be very careful because his father was very strong and would hurt us. We asked him how he know that it was his father that didn't want us in the attic and he said he snuck up to the attic after his father and saw him put something in the trunk and lock it. We asked him if he knew where the key was for the trunk and before he could answer the dark shadow started to appear and we stopped not wanting what happened during the seance to happen again."

Shelly called "I'm going to go to the children's room to see if I can make contact with Jacob again and see if he can tell me or show me where the key is" as she was going up stairs with Natasha on her heels.

"How's Mark?" Tina asked

"I'm not sure, how does church bells and birds singing sound to you" he said holding an ice pack to his head.

"Mark if you want to be excused from helping us any further, I would understand" Dr. Thomas said in a father son type fashion.

"Not on your life Doc, I'm having the time of my life. This is the greatest experience anybody could every ask for. Plus it will be something good to tell my grandchildren, if I ever have any" he said jokingly.

"It looks to me like we have one of the problems answered. We need to find out where Constance's baby was buried, if it was buried" Dr. Thomas said.

"Dr. Jefferson's friend never really told us anything about the bones".

"We don't have any way of telling who the bones belong to other than telling us it was a male, what race it was and maybe how old it was when it died."

Shelly and Natasha came downstairs and said that they couldn't get Jacob to come again. They felt that the dark shadow was not allowing him to come but they were not going to give up they will keep trying. They were going next into the basement and try communicating with Zachary. This time Tina, Shelly, Natasha and Vince all went. Maybe with all their combined efforts somebody will come across and tell us what they want us to do to stop the hauntings.

By the time they came back upstairs from the basement it was almost midnight and Dr. Jefferson had not returned yet.

We inquired as to whether they were able to communicate with Zachary and they said that he couldn't come either that the dark shadow was holding him back to.

I suggest that we all retire and try again tomorrow and maybe when Dr. Jefferson comes back he will have more information for us to go on and then maybe we can put an end to all of this.

Chapter 10

I was surprised that nothing happened during the night and that morning we all enjoyed an undisturbed breakfast. Everybody was busy doing the things that they needed to do for the day and I just sat there at the breakfast table drinking my coffee. I was half tempted to go out to the stone circle but thought better of it. That is a matter that can wait until we get the house cleared.

This morning Jonathan, Dr. Thomas and Vince were all out in the cemetery touching the headstones and walking around talking. I wondered what was going on but again I thought better of going out to see. I was glad to see that Vince had stopped sulking about not getting his way about the stone circle, but every once in a while I will see him standing staring in the direction of the circle.

Natasha was having a great time with the girls doing their psychic thing. I was glad she stayed, she helps me be strong when I feel like falling apart.

Mark, who recovered quite well, was working with Jason on their equipment getting it ready for the next bout that we were going to go through.

It was almost noon before Dr. Jefferson showed up. He had the boys help him unload some boxes from his car. He looked like he hadn't slept all night. I handed him a cup of coffee which he took a long drink from and handed it back to me.

"Thank you. I have lots to tell all of you. Boys go and find everybody, I'm too tired to tell this story more than one time. Have them all gather in the dinning room, please and thank you" he said in one breath.

"Come, I want you to see this before anybody else. It seems that my great grandfather fathered two children and one was your great-great aunt. After he left here he was heart broken. He met a lady named Patricia one night in a small down not far from here and they got married. Anyway, she gave birth to a child, who later met and married your great-great uncle, so you are related to my family in sort of a round about way."

Before I could answer everybody came in the door.

"What's up, did you learn anything?" Mark asked sitting down next to a large stack of boxes peaking inside.

"The historian was very helpful. She indicated that my great grandfather did leave here but settled in a small town not far from here, which isn't there anymore by the way, but he continued practicing medicine and was good at it. He met another lady in this town married her and had children with her and one child moved to the city to get away from the country life. This part has to do with Amy. As it was the child grew up and married Amy's great-great uncle Peter. So she is related to my side of the family in a way. I found several more diaries in the house that indicated that my great grandfather tried to communicate with Constance after he left but she wouldn't or couldn't respond. He sent letters to Angela which let her know what he had been doing but he never heard back from her either. I'm wondering if Nathaniel kept the letters from the ladies. Anyway, he mentioned in one of his diaries that Constance was keeping a diary that Nathaniel didn't know about that had a lot of information about what was going on here and that she wanted to use it to blackmail Nathaniel into telling her the truth about her baby. He did write that on one occasion she did see him and his wife in town once and she started crying and ran off. I wonder if she was jealous and it is she that is trying to get revenge in a round about way. But the story about her death is different, I thought that she died before he left but according to my grand fathers diaries she lived for some time after he left."

"I wonder if Constance's diary is in the trunk in the attic that the dark shadow is protecting so strongly?" I asked.

"Well the only way to find out is to go up there get the trunk and see what is in it". Dr. Jefferson said.

"That theory is all good and well, but last night Mark and I tried that and needless to say, Mark has a good size headache because of it".

"There is safety in numbers. I am all for going back up there. Some of us can divert the shadow, if it shows up, and the others can get the trunk out of the attic" Jason said.

"It's worth a try" Jonathan said.

So we all headed toward the attic. As we were going up the stairs the wind started howling, inside the house. There weren't any windows open because it was cold last night and I made sure they were closed. It was getting colder in the house as we made our way to the attic door. We were all shivering when we opened the door. It was like going out in an arctic storm.

"There's the trunk" I shouted, pointing at it.

"Ok, Vince help me move this thing" Jonathan said bending over the trunk.

As Vince started moving forward the dark shadow showed up again. Things were being thrown at all of us but this time we were able to knock them aside trying to protect Jonathan and Vince while they got the trunk.

"It's too heavy, Mark, Jason come help" Jonathan yelled.

The dark shadow screamed "Noooo" and started grabbing at the guys. They were able to dodge the shadow and finally got the trunk lifted and was moving for the door.

"We are not afraid of you any more. I demand that you leave this house. In the name of the father, the son and the holy spirit I demand that you leave my house"

"You can't command me" the voice boomed. It was very hard to stand up against the gust of wind from the voice, but I held my ground.

From behind me I heard someone yelling, the trunk is out, get out of there.

"I will get you out of my house one way or another" I screamed just as a several objects were hurtled at me, ducking to avoid being hit, I turned and ran for the door.

The door slammed in front of my face. I grabbed the handle trying to get the door opened but it wouldn't open. I screamed banging on the door for someone to open the door but hard as they tried nobody could get the door open. The dark shadow was right on me and I scrambled to get out of its way.

"I warned you. I am stronger than you" I heard the shadow bellowing.

Tripping and falling over trunks, boxes and other things, I found the doll that I had seen in my dream. Grabbing it and thinking maybe this would stop it, I kissed it and throw it at the shadow. It hit the shadow, it let out this blood curdling scream and disappeared. The doll fell to the floor with a thump. All went quite and the door opened. Everybody was standing at the door staring at me. I bent over, shaking like a leaf, and picked up the doll and headed for the door.

"Let's get that dam trunk downstairs and get it opened now" I said walking past everybody, trying control myself because I was on the verge of tears and half scared out of my mind.

It was not an easy thing getting that heavy trunk down but the guys did get it to the bottom of the stairs before saying, it wasn't going any farther, if I wanted to open it, it would have to be right there.

Still holding the doll I reached for the trunk and then this white mist appeared from behind the trunk and just as suddenly vanished.

"Get that trunk opened fast, I think the dark shadow may show up at any time" Dr. Thomas said.

The lock on the trunk was stuck. We had to pry it open. Finally it gave way.

Inside the trunk we found a skeleton fully clothed. The clothes it had on were of the same era as the ones Nathaniel has on in the large portrait over the staircase. We turned the turn on its side and the body fell out. A gold pocket watch fell out from the jacket. Jonathan picked it up and read the inscription on the back.

"To my darling Morgan, Love Angela"

Behind the skeleton was a large bundle wrapped in rags and a smaller bundle wrapped in paper. Dr. Thomas picked up the small bundle and laid it on the carpet in front of the trunk and started to unwrap the large bundle but the dark shadow showed up.

"No" it screamed, slamming the trunk against a wall.

"It's too late, you can't stop us now" I screamed back.

All of the sudden the dark shadow was all over Jonathan and took possession of his body. He struggled to try to get it off, gasping and fell to the floor. His features started changing, his face became distorted. When he opened his eyes they glowed red like the gates of hell and he had the look of total hatred on his face. He stood up struggling to breath, he could feel the creature inside his body and mind taking control of him. He could taste its foul, dank, rancid, ghastly breath filling his lungs. He gagged and coughed trying to expel. It was no use he no longer was in control and was compelled to do the creatures bidding.

"I told you not to open that trunk. I told you, you were not welcome in this house. I told you someone was going to get killed" the entity inside Jonathan said.

Mark, Vince and Jason moved but Jonathan lashed out at them with his arm tossing them aside like rag dolls.

"You have no right opening that trunk" he yelled.

Dr. Thomas had unwrapped the small bundle and found it was letters from Morgan to Angela.

"You killed Morgan and hid him in the trunk didn't you? That's why the haunting is going on in this house, he's out for revenge" I yelled.

He lurched for me. The men tried to restrain him but it was no good, they were thrown aside like paper sacks. Grabbing the bundles we ladies ran out of th house as fast as possible. Soon after the guys came out of the house, bruised and bloodied.

We gathered outside under the large tree on the other side of the driveway looking back at the house. We could see Jonathan staring back at us through the windows. Maybe Nathaniel's spirit couldn't cross the threshold, maybe he is confined to the house, if it was Nathaniel's spirit controlling Jonathan. That would be good for us, at lease we were safe outside. The sounds emitting from the house were horrifying. It was as if there were 100 people in there screaming at the top of their lungs while they tore up the place. Vince said he could feel several spirits moving about in the house now and we were helpless to get rid of them, for now.

Dr. Jefferson stood there looking at the house with this exasperated look on his face.

"How can it be Morgan's body? He moved away, unless his love for Angela was so strong he came back and Nathaniel caught them together and killed him, or them. I did find an article in the local newspaper, that his wife had reported him missing and there was a massive search but nobody found him".

He fell silent and stared at the cemetery, I wondered if he was thinking the same thing I was thinking, check Angela's grave to see if she was really buried there or if she was also stuffed in a trunk somewhere in the house.

"What are we going to do?" I looked at everybody and asked. Nobody responded.

"Looks like we need an exorcism and I know just the guy who can help us" Jason said and with that he picked up his phone.

"I can't leave Jonathan in there" I said starting back to the house.

Dr. Thomas grabbed me holding me back. "It is not Jonathan that is in there. It may be his body but the entity that is possessing him is dangerous. As long as we stay out he will not hurt Jonathan, so we have to regroup and come up with a plan that will get rid of the entity without hurting Jonathan".

"Jonathan didn't believe in ghosts" I said with a slight laugh but nobody laughed with me.

"I'm going to try to sneak back into the house. I just had a premonition from Zachary, he wants to help" Vince said.

"You can't go back in there by yourself" Natasha said getting up and grabbing his arm.

"Ah, Nat, I have been through worse, I can't remember right now when, but I know I can contact Zachary to see how he can help us" he responded.

"Well if you're going in there, I'm going with you" Natasha said stubbornly.

"Me to" said Shelly.

"Don't count me out" said Tina.

"It's not safe for to many people to go in there" Dr Jefferson said.

"Wait, I know how they can get in without Jonathan or the entities seeing them. Through the barn. Follow me".

When we got to the barn I showed them through Jonathan's workshop and then to back where the little room with the trap door in the floor was.

"Go down through there, it will bring you out into the cellar.

Here, you will need flashlights. Be quite when you go through the tunnel, even though it is dirt there, it still has an echoing effect. Please be careful" I said.

Vince winked at me as he led the way in to the dark abyss.

The door to the cellar was not locked and Vince quietly opened it and stepped out. Almost immediately he felt Zachary's presence. The girls followed and felt him also.

"Zachary" Vince whispered. "Zachary, we are here. I know you want to help, please give me a sign that it is you and not the evil entity upstairs".

Zachary materialized and told them to seek the secret in the attic wall. He didn't tell them what it was or which wall it was in, but he said it would put an end to Nathaniel's rage and to take the doll with us for protection.

"Zachary, you need to go to the light. Topieta is waiting for you there" Tina said several times.

"Not done" he said and he was gone.

They made their way back through the tunnel and after wiping off the dirt and dust from themselves and told us what we were supposed to do.

"But how are we going to get into the attic without "it" seeing us and stopping us?"

I asked.

"Wait a minute, there are secret passages in the walls" Dr. Jefferson replied.

"Yes, but I have never explored them. There wasn't time before all this started happening" I replied.

"Well, my great grandfather said in his diaries that he used to go from floor to floor to see Angela in secret passages when Nathaniel was drunk and if he could do it, why couldn't we?"

"I'm all for it. Do you know what passages he used?"

"No, but it will be exciting to see what is in there. I have wondered about them many times. Once before Jonathan's grandmother passed away, I almost asked her if I could explore the old house, but I thought that would be intruding on her privacy so I didn't. Now I wish I had" Dr. Jefferson said.

"There's a secret panel in the kitchen cupboard inside the pantry. I found it one day when I was straightening up and accidently fell grabbing on a hanger on the wall. When the door opened it scared me and I never went in".

That is where Dr. Jefferson, Tina, Natasha and Vince headed for. Natasha was holding onto the doll with white knuckles. She turned and looked at me giving me a wink and crocked smile as she disappeared inside the wall, closing it quietly behind her.

"I think we should wait outside just in case Jonathan comes in here" Dr. Thomas whispered, and with that the rest of us went outside.

I never noticed the outside of the house like this before but there were sculptured windows where there weren't any rooms. I wondered if they were put there to light up the secret passage ways, before I could finish the thought I saw the Vince passing by one of the windows, my question was answered. At least they are not in total darkness in those passages.

"Hey, doc, how are we going to tell which wall to look in if we can't make any noise?" Vince whispered.

Dr. Jefferson stopped, thought for a moment.

"Well, I haven't figured that one out just yet, but I did read my great grandfather's diary, which I have with me, which has a map of the passage ways so maybe I'll find something there that says which wall we need to be interested in".

"But how are we going to get into the wall without any tools and without making any noise?"

"I don't know. Wait until we get there will you!"

They came to a staircase that led them farther upwards. As they passed any kind of a panel that led to the outside Dr. Jefferson quietly peered out to see where they were. After several stops they finally came to the hallway which lead to the attic.

"Well, my friends we are here but not in the attic, so we

may have to go one by one to make sure nobody or nothing sees us".

Dr. Jefferson went first. The door to the attic creaked as he started to open it, hesitating for a second to make sure nobody heard it, he pushed the door slowly open and indicated to the others to follow him. After they all were inside Dr. Jefferson closed the door and locked it.

"Maybe that will keep Jonathan out until we find what we are looking for" he whispered.

They hadn't been in the attic long before they heard a squeaking sound coming from the hall. As quickly and quietly as they could they hid, hoping that Jonathan wasn't coming to the attic to check on things. Breathlessly they waited. Minutes seemed to pass and nothing happened.

Dr. Jefferson signaled that it should be safe to start tapping the walls. Going from wall to wall they tapped to see if there were any hollow spots, finally Vince found a spot in the wall closet to the door. Feeling the wall he indicated that there was a panel that moved, using his pocket knife he pried the panel open. Giving way with a slight creaking sound, out came a small book.

"Let's get back downstairs and outside before we open it. It could bring Jonathan or something else in here and we don't want and/or need that right now" Dr. Jefferson whispered as he quietly unlocked the door.

Just as he started to open the door, it burst open. There was Jonathan looking like a wild crazy man.

"Give me that" he said pointing at Vince.

"Not on your life" he said tossing the package to Natasha and the book to Tina.

The girls took the cue, tossing the package and the book so Jonathan couldn't get it they moved toward the door and escape.

"Sorry to do this old buddy" Vince said as he hit Jonathan, knocking him out. He closed the door and took off his belt, tied one end around the door handle and the other to the banister, then ran to catch up with the others.

They scrambled down the stairs and out the back door. They looked half scared when they came crashing out the back door.

"We got it" Tina yelled running. "Let's get out of here before Jonathan comes to and go someplace safe before we open it".

"Let's go to my house" Dr. Jefferson said out of breath.

"What do you mean comes to?" I asked Vince.

"I decked him so we could get out. He's ok" he replied rubbing his knuckles.

I hesitated wondering if I should go into tend to Jonathan, he could be back to normal. As I started toward the house Vince grabbed my arm.

"Look honey, I know that you're concerned about Jonathan, but the best thing to do right now is to leave him alone and come with us. Maybe my hitting him and knocking him out knocked the entity out of him and he'll be ok when he wakes up".

"What if that creature takes over his body permanently and he's never normal again?" I cried, tears running down my face.

Vince took me in his strong arms and held me until I finished crying and took my tear stained face in his hands.

"Don't you worry about that, I'll make sure that Jonathan is ok and he'll be back to his loving self before this is through, I promise" he said looking gently in my eyes and kissed my forehead.

Dr. Jefferson came up right at that time and said "Look, we don't have all night. Let's get out of here".

Chapter 11

At Dr. Jefferson's house we all gathered in his large sitting room. Setting the package, the large bundle, the book and the doll on the coffee table we all sat there just looking at it in silence.

When Dr. Jefferson finally spoke it scared all of us. When he opened the large bundle there were the bones of small child.

"Oh God" he said.

"Could that be the bones of Constance's baby?"

"It's possible. The only way to tell is through DNA or maybe one of the spirits will came and claim it. But for now, I'll put it in a small box so that it can be buried properly later".

"We are going to have to take the bones of my great grand-father to the cemetery and give him a proper burial also. Maybe that will stop some of the spirits." Dr. Jefferson said.

"We will soon. But we need to concentrate on getting Jona-than out of the house and clear the house of the spirits. I fear that somebody is going to get hurt and I don't know how to stop it". Dr. Thomas said.

"Maybe we should open the package to see what is in there don't you think?" he said reaching for the package.

"Maybe Amy should be the one to open it. She is the one that really needs to know what is going on" Vince said, looking at me with a very caring look on his face.

My hand was shaking as I reached for the package. When I controlled myself enough to open the book, I could tell from the writing it was done by a female. It must be Constance's diary. It gave me the cold chills to hold it.

"Before we read the book we need to find out as much about Nathaniel and Angela as we possibly can. We need to check to see if there are any historical records we haven't read to see if there is something in them that may help us explain what is going on in your house Amy" Shelly said.

"I have Angela's diary and some letters but that is all I have other than the trunks and boxes full of pictures in the attic. Wait a minute I have a locket, I'll have to go to my bedroom and get it. But how I am going to get back in the house without Jonathan catching me. Maybe he has calmed down by now and I can just walk right in and not have anything to fear?" I said looking questioningly at Dr. Jefferson.

"We have to get in that attic and if there is anything else in there that I can find, I need to look at and/or read as much as I can before we open this new book. I know it may not be the possible answer to what is going on, but it is best to know as much as possible about your "ghosts" before trying to exorcize them. Give me the book and the letters, I will red them first before going exploring any more. Maybe the book can tell us exactly what happened to Morgan" Shelly said.

Constance's diary talked about how she was being abused not only by Nathaniel but also by Zachary. Both men told her that if she didn't do what they wanted and if she spoke to anybody about what was happening, they would let their slave

Magumba, and extremely large, very heavy set male, have his way with her so she had to give into every whim they had. All the time she was plotting and scheming a way to get revenge on both men.

She spoke of Dr. Morgan who was a kind and gentle person, whom she had instantly taken a liking to but he didn't notice her, he only had eyes for Angela.

"How could he want her, she already has a husband. If I tell Nathaniel what I know maybe he will leave me alone" she wrote. Next entry said "Dear Diary, I am with child. It has to be Nathaniel's because Zachary has not be with me for several months now".

"The only way Morgan can continue coming here is to pretend he loves me and I will make him do so or I will tell Nathaniel what I know."

"Dear Diary I have agreed to marry Morgan. I did not tell him I am with child. I Laid with him on our wedding night. I will make him think it is his that way I can keep him."

"Morgan is away to attend to the sick, it is my time, the baby is coming. Lord I am so frightened. Nathaniel is in one of his wild rages tonight. I pray all goes well with the birthing"

"Dear Diary, Nathaniel has taken my baby away. He told me that it was born death. It can't be. I know I heard it crying."

"It has been a week and I still hear my baby crying in my dreams. Oh how I long to hold it. I wake nights also haring the sound of a baby. I follow the sound throughout the house and then to the cemetery but I still can't find my baby".

"Dear Diary, Morgan is plotting to take Angela away and I must find a way to stop them. How I have learned to hate my sister, I'll stop them if it is the last thing I do."

"I have fallen ill, dear diary. Angela and Morgan tend to me. Morgan, my sweet Morgan, he sits by my bed giving me tea and reading to me. Why am I so tired?"

"Today my hand maiden told me that Morgan has been

putting something in my tea and that I should not drink it. Tonight I will pretend to be asleep when Morgan comes and I will not drink the tea."

"I have refused the tea now for several days and I'm feeling better. I sit at my dressing table trying to think of a way to stop him. I swear I'll get even with him and Angela one way or the other."

That was the last entry in her diary.

"Now we know possibly who one of the mad entities around here might be" Shelly said.

All of the sudden she felt very cold and the shutters to her windows in her room slammed shut. She was in total darkness. When her eyes adjusted to the light she noticed a small glowing, growing mist out of the corner of her eye. She held her breath thinking that maybe whatever or whoever it was would leave if it didn't sense anybody in the room. No such luck, it kept getting bigger and bigger and started taking on the form of a woman.

"You have read my diary, I heard you, you must help me get revenge"

It was Constance.

"Kill Nathaniel".

"I will do no such thing. He's not Nathaniel, Nathaniel's dead. That is Jonathan not Nathaniel".

"It's the only way to stop him".

"There has to be some other way" Shelly pleaded.

"I want him dead. He is a seed of a monster".

"Jonathan is not a monster".

Before she could continue she was thrown across the room, smashing into the wall. Weakly she got up trying to catch her breath.

"I will do nothing to hurt Jonathan".

Again she was slammed into the wall.

"You will do as I tell you or I will kill you" Constance bellowed.

Shelly's mind was whirling, she couldn't think. She tried to get up again but she was being held down and she felt like she was being choked.

"Constance, Morgan did not betray you. He left because he was forced to by Nathaniel" Shelly said struggling for breath and trying to buy herself some time. With that the crushing feeling went away, but Constance did not leave.

"Nathaniel killed Morgan and hid his body in a trunk in the attic".

"I don't believe you" Constance cried.

A knock on the door brought the lights on and the shutters open. Shelly had just enough strength to get to the door, open it and then collapsed in a heap on the floor.

When she opened her eyes she was on her back staring at the ceiling. When she tried to get up her body hurt so bad she just laid still. From her right side she heard Amy say.

"Shelly what in the world happened to you?"

"Constance came to visit me. She said some awful things and even though I pleaded with her she didn't believe me. I have a feeling that Jonathan's life is in danger. I think it would be a good idea if when he's back to him normal self, you two go away and stay away until this thing is over."

"What are you talking about. I am not going anywhere. That is my house and I'm nothing is going to get me out of it." I said defiantly.

"Amy, Constance wants Jonathan dead. She said that he is a bad seed, spawned by the devil Nathaniel. I pleaded with her but she wouldn't listen. If ghosts have ears, that is. I even told her Nathaniel killed Morgan, but I really don't think she heard me. I really believe your live's are in danger here".

"I have all of you to protect me and Jonathan and I can take care of myself. Now let's get you up, we have a lot to do and little time to do it in" I said helping Shelly sit up.

"Ok, if you won't listen to me, at lease do not go off by yourself for any reason. There is protection in numbers. I am going to tell the others what happened here and what Constance wants, so don't be surprised if they agree with me about getting you out of here to safety" Shelly said putting on her sweater.

We didn't know it but Dr. Thomas had been listening to what we had been talking about and interjected, "Shelly is right Amy, if Constance has a nasty agenda or wants revenge she might go to great lengths to carry it out".

"Look, like I told Shelly, that is my house and I am not going to leave".

"Well if you come across any really cold spots in the house, go around them or get the hell out of there" Dr. Thomas said trying to make light of the situation.

Just then, Jason came in and said he had contacted his friend and priest, Father O'Malley and that he would be here soon to check out the house before he could perform an exorcism.

Chapter 12

When Father David O'Malley arrived at Dr. Jefferson's house we all took turns explaining to him our experiences, letting letter him know we have had contact with the dead, one that manifested and made demands on us and that there is one in particular that is strong enough to pick people up and throw them.

He didn't look like a priest, he had on a cowboy hat, a plaid shirt, levis and boots. When he took off his hat he was much younger than I though a priest should be, he looked no older than 25. His sandy blonde hair and deep green eyes made him look more lie a model than a priest. At first I wasn't sure he could do what we needed to do but when he started explaining things I knew better.

At first he was skeptical, which is understandable and expected, I would never have believed all of this if I hadn't been living it.

He said he wanted to go over to my house and see for himself whether or not what we are saying is true.

He had a strange look on his face when we drove up the driveway.

"I know this house. I remember performing a marriage ceremony here years ago. As I remember it, somebody had told me about disturbances here then also, but nothing ever came of it" he said.

The house looked like any ordinary plantation house, nothing was happening outside. The birds were singing, the last of the season butterflies were fluttering about, the sun was shining, I even saw a cat chasing something on the front porch. That is strange to see a cat because we don't own a cat.

Father O'Malley stepped on the porch, his breathing became very rapid and he started sweating. Upon entering the house, he started having hallucinations and speaking in languages I've never heard. As we watched from the windows, he was turned around by unseen hands so quickly that I thought he broke his neck. He was being forced out of the house, moving like his whole body was stiff, none of his joints bents as he was being moved across the floor. Just as he reached the door, he was thrown into the yard and the door slammed shut.

Scrambling to get to him both doctors checked him out to see if he was breathing and to make sure he was comfortable until he regained consciousness. He came to a few minutes later. He said that whatever it is in there was confusing him, giving him false memories of his childhood, even made him see himself in past lives. That there was one particular evil spirit trying to alter his thoughts and perceptions of God.

"Well, Father do you believe now?"

"I know that there is something in that house and I will do whatever it takes to help you get rid of it. I will need a couple of days to prepare. Jason, I'll need your help. It is ok to borrow him for a couple of days isn't it Dr. Thomas?" He asked.

"Yes. When you two return we will meet at Dr. Jefferson's

house and you can explain to us what you are going to do and how we can help."

I slipped away after everybody had go to bed and snuck back to my house. As I was looking into the windows I saw Jonathan sitting in the large chair in the living room. His eyes were huge, they darted from side to side watching for anything to move. His head jerked as if he was a robot on guard against trespassers. I thought he saw me which scared me and I ran like hell to get back to Dr. Jefferson's house.

When Jason and Father O'Malley came back I was extremely anxious to get back to the house to check on Jonathan.

Father explained that since maybe only one entity had possession of Jonathan we would need to somehow restrain him so he could try to exorcize the demon first and then start work on the house.

"Amy, I want you to know that doing an exorcism is very dangerous, not only to us but to Jonathan as well. You will have to be very strong, your belief in the almighty will have to be strong and you will have to have complete faith in me. You will need to have control at all times and tell Jonathan that you love him and want him to come back to you. Do you understand? Here are the prayers I will be using. Try to memorize them, or keep them close so you can say them with me. The stronger everyone's faith is the better chance we have."

"When do you want to get started?" I asked.

"First thing in the morning. Tonight we need to come up with a plan to restrain Jonathan".

Morning came and nobody felt like breakfast, so after explaining how the guys were going to handle Jonathan, we headed for the house. They found Jonathan still sitting in the large chair I had seen him in the other night. Vince entered the house and headed straight for the living room He entered from the front of the house while the others entered from the back.

"Hey, ole buddy how's it going?" Vince asked nonchalantly.

"Get out" demanded the voice.

"Now that's no way to treat a friend who came over just to see how you were doing, is it?"

"Get out" came the voice louder as Jonathan stirred in the chair.

"Hey, look Jon I need you to see this my way, I came down here because you asked me for help and I don't like the way you are treating me."

The other slowly crept into the room heading for the back of the chair, trying to get there without Jonathan seeing them.

"I SAID GET OUT!" the voice came again deafening.

"You'll have to make me" Vince said defiantly.

The words had just left his lip when Jonathan leapt from the chair, but before he could hit the ground there were several ropes around his body. It took all five men to tackle him, wrestle him to the ground and get him securely tied up. Then Dr. Jefferson injected him with a sedative to knock him out.

When Jonathan came to he was securely bound and sitting in a chair in the middle of the living room. We had removed all the furniture in order to keep them from being destroyed during the exorcism process.

When Father O'Malley came into the room his appearance had drastically changed. He was dressed in his ceremonial robes. He seemed to have aged over night, he looked so focused, centered and concerned about what was going to take place. He handed crucifixes to all of us, blessing them as he handed them out, telling us to wear them during the exorcism.

"Keep in mind that whatever Jonathan says or does it is not him but the entity that controls him".

He started by sprinkling holy water and saying the basic blessings from his bible. The entity only laughed and called him a fool, saying he was in control and nothing was going to remove him now.

Shelly chimed in by sprinkling a purified salt and water solution and chanted her own blessings.

"I banish you from this house, you wicked, evil thing. Be

cone I command you. I compel you to leave this house. Return here never more. Go back to hell where you belong" she said.

With all of us praying, Shelly chanting and Father O'Malley sprinkling holy water as he prayed the entity screamed and laughed at us.

"Jonathan you have to let us help you. You need to command this thing to leave your body and return to where it came. You have the power within you."

"Jonathan, it's Amy, I love you, come back to me".

As the entity shouted profanity at us there was a sudden drop in the room temperature and blood started oozing and dripping from the windows and the walls, the ceiling cracked and blood started dripping on us from there also.

"Jonathan tell it to leave, tell it to cross over into the light, we need your help to close the portal on this entity now" Father O'Malley shouted wiping the blood from his face.

"You're dead! You have to go! Go into the light. Set Jonathan free. Leave this house" I screamed.

Again the high pitched screams came from inside Jonathan, contorting his face wickedly, his breathing had turned into panting and slobber started flowing from his mouth.

"You must go. Get out of my house" I couldn't help myself I said with tears streaming down my face.

See my weakness the entities voice turned into that of Jonathan "Amy, come to me, I want to hold you, honey". I started to go to him but Father O'Malley stopped me.

"If you go to him he will kill you. Don't give into temptation, it is not Jonathan talking".

The entity bellowed again, "Come my pretty, I need to have your body next to mine".

"Go to hell" I screamed.

A wind inside the room started kicking up and was getting pretty intense, we could hardly stand up right, the only way to communicate now was to yell at each other. Father O'Malley kept praying and sprinkling holy water. Every drop that landed on the floor steamed as if the floor was made of hot coals.

"This house is pure evil. I don't know if I can banish this entity" he yelled at us with fear in his voice.

"You have to try Father. I have faith in you" I yelled back at him.

Then he pulled out his book on exorcism and stood as tall as he could and stated in a very loud and confident voice.

"Heavenly Father, we acknowledge your presence in our lives and you are here with us today. You are all-powerful and you know all things. We need you, and we know that we can do nothing without you. We ask that you help us to remove this entity that is lost here on earth and remove it from this poor sole and this house. We ask for your guidance to help the spirit, give it the power to find happiness and peace and to move on to the other side. In the name of God and Jesus, we ask your help in releasing this entity from the earthly bound plane. We ask the Holy Spirit's help in releasing the entity form the earth bound plane. In the name of God I banish you. In the name of Jesus I banish you. In the name of the Holy Spirit I banish you. In the name of Christ I compel you to leave".

Then he made the sign of the cross with holy water on Jonathan's forehead, placed his hands on his face and the bible on his heart and continued.

"In the name of Jesus I compel you evil one to leave, in the name of Jehovah I compel you to leave, in the name of Jesus I compel you to leave, in the name of Christ I compel you to leave" he said repeating this several times, each time his voice was louder and louder.

The entity inside Jonathan struggled against the feel of the priest's hands on him. He cursed the priest, spuing forth profanity.

Jonathan looked over at Tina and she screamed and clutched her chest.

"Leave her alone" Shelly screamed and through red brick

dust on Jonathan. Only after he looked away could Tina remove her hands from her chest and she collapsed. Jason and Mark grabbed her before he hit the floor and helped her up.

"It felt like red hot fingers clutching my heart. It felt like it was going to burst" she said struggling to breath.

Tina recovered and yelled at Jonathan.

"Jonathan you need to tell the entity you're not afraid of it. Tell it to leave".

Jonathan struggled against the ropes, rocking back and forth in the chair. The veins on his face protruded like there were going to pop. Profanity poured from his mouth like water. One minute his eyes were coal black. They looked like eyes of a shark when it attacks. The next minute they were fire red. Father reassured me that the entity needed him to exist and wouldn't let him die.

Before we started trying to exorcize Jonathan I had brought the doll and Angela's locket into the room, setting them on the window sill. I remembered what had happened in the attic when I threw the doll at the dark shadow.

"Father, I'm going to try something" I yelled showing him the doll and the locket.

He looked at me questioningly. I headed toward Jonathan holding the doll and the locket in front of me, slowly at first, looking at his eyes all the while. His eyes stared at me, and then the doll and then the locket. As I inched closer his eyes got bigger and bigger. He started struggling more fiercely against the ropes, spitting at me, cursing more and more with each step I took.

"Jonathan I love you. Come back to me. Entity I command you to leave Jonathan and never return to this world. In the name of Jesus Christ I command you to leave" I yelled as I moved closer and closer.

I suddenly rushed forward, pressed the doll to Jonathan's heart and the locket to his forehead. He let out a deafening scream and went limp.

A great white light covered the room and like a blast of hot air threw everybody against the walls across the room.

Chapter 13

When we came to Jonathan was slumped over in the chair. I started to go to him but Mark grabbed my arm.

"It may not be safe" he whispered.

Father O'Malley went over to Jonathan and cautiously touched his head. Jonathan stirred and Father jumped like he had been shot.

"Wow, man I have such a headache" Jonathan said lifting his head and sitting up in the chair.

"Jonathan" I said as I ran to him.

"Why am I tied up? Get me out of these things" he demanded.

I grabbed at them but Father stopped me.

"First, I must be sure the demon is gone"

"What demon?" Jonathan asked.

Father O'Malley laid his crucifix on Jonathan and nothing happened, he made a cross with holy water on his forehead and still nothing happened.

"I believe that the entity has gone and the exorcism worked" he said proudly.

It took the about three quarters of an hour to explain what had happened before Jonathan understood whey he was tied up.

"Ok, Amy let's pull out all the stops and get rid of this ghosts once and for all" Jonathan finally said.

We retreated to Dr. Jefferson's house for the night just to be on the safe side and to make plans on how to rid the house of the ghosts.

The next day we gathered together all the stuff we thought we would need to cleanse the house. I was hopeful that this would do it but I knew in my heart that it would probably not work, but it was worth a try.

We went back to our house and each of use took turns sprinkling holy water and powdered sandalwood (Shelly's idea) on the ground while we prayed and walked clockwise around the outside of the house and all the buildings on the place, including the cemetery. Natasha, Tina and Shelly all chanted blessing and protection prayers as we walked from around the barn and the old slave quarters. They explained that by doing this the entities in these buildings will be confined there and we can exorcism them easier that way when we get the main house cleansed. They were hoping once the main house was cleansed it will release all the trapped spirits and they will move on by themselves.

Jonathan wanted to put salt on the ground but because there were lots of plants and trees around, I told him that it would kill them and they didn't do anything to us. So eh conceded with my wishes. All the while this was going on, I was holding on to the doll and wearing Angela's locket. I remembered what happened in the attic so I though they would protect me.

We were surprised that nothing happened while we ere blessing the buildings. Vince, Mark, Shelly, Natasha and Tina all went into the barn and slave quarters and said that there were no entities or spirits in them. So we concentrated on the main house.

Father O'Malley said a prayer of blessing and sprinkled holy water on us, praying that nothing should happen to any of use in this fight against evil and with that we went inside.

As we opened the front door we could see things swirling around in the air and thing were thrown at the door smashing into it. Father O'Malley said that we needed to find the main source where the entities entered the house, the portal if you will, and send the entities back through it.

"Jason get your gages and see if you can find the coldest spot in the house, but be extra careful not to get hit by flying objects and if you see any entities, get the heck out of there. When you find it, if you find it, that will be the portal that we must concentrate on" Dr. Thomas told him.

Jonathan said that he had a feeling that the cemetery had something to do with what is going on in the house.   He couldn't put his finger on it but he said he needed to go to Nathaniel's grave. Vince, Natasha and I followed him there while the others stayed in the house to find the portal.

Jonathan walked up to the monument of his great grandfather and placed his hands on it. Vince looked at him puzzled.

"He's not psychic, what does he think he is doing?"

"Leave him alone and let him do what he thinks he needs to do" I snapped at Vince.

Jonathan turned around and said we need to find a way to open the tomb.

"Why?" I asked, frightened of what we might unleash.

"I have to see if he's in there or not."

"Jonathan what if he is and his spirit is unleashed, if he hasn't already been unleashed, like the ones in the house? Couldn't that be dangerous?"

"Look are you going to help me or not?"

With that we all started feeling around to see if there may be a hidden latch or something. By accident Jonathan stripped pulling down on the stirrup and the front of the tomb door cracked open. Spuing out rancid air and dust.

We entered very cautiously, in the room was this huge coffin which had the lid carelessly placed on top of it. Jonathan walked up to the coffin and slid the top off. We gasp as the sight. His great grandfather's corpse had been savagely crushed. It looked like somebody had on purposely destroyed his corpse. The clothes he had been wearing when he was buried were all ripped and torn. There was a very large knife sticking out of his ribs. Natasha brushed against the wall and turning around to brush herself off noticed that there was writing on the wall. She brushed off the cob webs to reveal "I hated you in life. I hate you in death".

"Wow, I wonder if it's our great grandmother causing all that is happening in the house" I asked Jonathan, who was still looking at the corpse.

"What? Oh, ah, she wouldn't do that, would she" he ask still looking at the corpse.

"Jonathan, we need to look at your great grandmother's diary again and maybe even her coffin to see if there are clues in there that could help us solve this" Vince said as he started toward the door.

"Help me put the lid back on. Respect for the dead you know" Jonathan said trying to lift the lid by himself.

Once back in the house I tried to remember where I had put the diary. The house was still in disarray, the things were still swirling about and things were still being thrown at us. Mark who had been reading the diary walked in the room just then. Vince asked if he could read it and Mark handed it to him. He immediately started reading as fast as he could.

Just then a stranger came to the door, his eyes were wide with astonishment and disbelief. It was the man that had car trouble that stormy night. Only this time he was dressed in a very nice grey suit.

"I told you I was here for a special purpose" he called to me from the door.

I moved closer to the door and asked "Who are you?"

"My great grandmother was Topieta, love of Zachary Chamberlain".

Once he said that and stepped inside the house everything stopped. Everything that had been flying around fell to the ground with a deafening crash, the wind stopped blowing. It was quite, almost too quite. We were almost afraid to move for fear it would start up again. I stepped outside on the veranda, motioning for him to follow me.

Dr. Jefferson came over to the stranger as asked "Who are you, young man?"

"David Zachary Chamberlain" he said proudly.

"Your great grandmother was Topieta?" I asked.

"Yes"

"Everybody thought she had been killed before she gave birth" Jonathan said walking up to shake his hand. "I'm Jonathan Chamberlain, Zachary was my great uncle. What are you doing here?"

"Well as I stated my great grandmother was Topieta and yes she was killed by a slave trader but before she died she gave birth to my grandfather and from what I understand she insisted that the baby have the last name of Chamberlain, that of his father. Because the slave trader also loved her, he kept the baby and raised him as his own. He sent my grandfather to the best schools and told him the complete story of Topieta's file, as he knew it. I did some searching in lots and lots of archived material and found out where she had been prior to being sen to the slave traders camp and found out about your great uncle. I was surprised that there were any records still in existence. So here I am back to where it all started".

"Did you notice how everything stopped flying around when he said his name. I wonder if Topieta may have something to do with what is happening here? Dr. Thomas asked.

"How could that be, she was killed, sorry David, so far away from here. How could her spirit come back here to raise such a ruckus?" I asked.

"My grandfather told me that Topieta loved this place very much and that is why she and Zachary wanted to be married, not because of the baby, but because he made her feel like she belonged here. She loved Zachary very much. My great grandmother's body was supposed to have been brought back here secretly and buried in the cemetery, next to Zachary. That is why I came back here. I wanted to have her body moved to the family plot so all our relatives can take care of it like we should".

"David, we don't know if she was buried here. There are no markers in the cemetery for her" Jonathan said looking in the direction of the cemetery.

Just then Vince came up and said he found something in the diary.

"I was feeling the cover of the diary and found this little slot with a letter from Angela to Topieta's family in it. So her family must have been here on the plantation also. It says that her body had been brought back without Nathaniel knowing about it per Zachary's request, but that when she and Dr. Jefferson were trying to bury her Nathaniel showed up and stole her body and hit it from them".

"That bastard" Jonathan said.

"Jonathan, maybe her body is somewhere in the house, like the attic, and that maybe what the dark figure doesn't want us to find it and maybe that is why it is so protective of the attic".

"We have to get up there and tear that place apart, let no box, crate or trunk go unturned to see if we can find her" Jonathan said starting toward the stairs.

Before he could take two steps the house erupted in kaos. Grabbing a chair to shield myself I raced for the stairs. As I stepped on the stairs they buckled under my feet and a gapping hole opened up and I fell through to the basement.

Jonathan was the first to reach me to see if I was hurt. Stunned I got up. Surprisingly I wasn't hurt.

"Let's get to the attic" I said running up the stairs with Jonathan right behind me.

Being careful to step over the broken steps we finally made our way to the first landing. The picture of Nathaniel came alive and he started grabbing at us. Jason was the first to get caught and started thrashing him around. The guys all tried to get him free.

"Get to the attic, I'll be ok" he yelled.

Jonathan, Vince, Mark, David and I ran for the attic while the other stayed to help Jason. I could hear someone scream but I kept on running.

The door to the attic was covered in a thick layer of slim, it was oozing from the cracks of the door facing. Vince had some how brought with him a sledge hammer and started slamming away at the door. Finally it gave in. We grabbed boxes, crates and trunks opening them and throwing the contents all out on the floor. We had gone through all of the stuff and found nothing.

"Jonathan I wonder if maybe her body could be hidden inside the wall. Zachary did say look inside the wall" Vince said holding the sledge hammer.

"Be my guest, have at it".

It wasn't long before he stopped. Topieta's body was hidden inside the wall. The temperature in the room suddenly dropped to freezing and the room went dark. We could see an eerie glow coming from inside the wall where Topieta's body was. The glow grew brighter and brighter. All of the sudden the dark figure showed up. We hid as best we could so maybe it wouldn't see us. This beautiful white mist appeared and took hold of the very large candle stick which was onto of one of the trunk, and it started levitating, moving toward the dark figure. The mist took on the shape of a woman, as it became move visible it took on the shape of Topieta. The dark figure turned into Nathaniel.

"You killed me. I have waited all these years for somebody to release me so I could take my revenge on you".

"You bitch, I'll kill those who set you free" he yelled at her.

She didn't flinch. Like a flash she was on Nathaniel hitting him with the candle stick. He roared each time the candle stick hit him. It was awful, each time she hit him his head split open. This black, icky, runny stuff, that smell like hell, came running out of the wounds. As she hit him the stuff flew all over the walls, floors and all over us. With one last blow she hit him so hard that he exploded, blowing out the windows and throwing us all over everywhere. Mark had been thrown thru one of the windows, Vince had been thrown so hard that he hit the ceiling with his head and landed on the floor with a loud thump.

Unfortunately Mark who had been thrown through the window landed head first on one of the stone statues in the front yard breaking his neck. Dr. Jefferson was first to reach him, after checking his pulse, he took off his jacket and placed it over him.

Shelly came running out of the house and screamed "No" and fainted.

Jonathan turned and yelled at the house "I'm going to burn that house to the ground and sew the ground with salt so nothing can every grow here again" and stormed toward the front door.

Tina cried "That won't stop the evil that's going on in there. It will just make matters worse Jonathan".

Jonathan stopped, turned and looked at her "How can things get worse?" pointing at Mark's body.

"Hear her out Jon. She is right. I feel it to, there is still something evil here that need to be reckoned with. I don't know what it is, but I know we are close to finding out and then we can end all of this" Vince said trying to make Jonathan understand.

When we went back inside the house Topieta's ghost was still there, waiting.

"Thank you for setting me free" she said with a smile.

Just then Zachary's ghost appeared, she smiled at him, reaching for him. As they embraced a great white light appeared above them, they waived to us and then vanished into the light.

"Wait your great grandson is here and he wants to see you" I called, but they were gone.

"David we will help you gather your great grandmothers remains so that you can take them with you for a proper burial" Jonathan said.

"Now I can lay her to rest with the rest of the family, in the family plot back home" he said with tears in his eyes.

The doctors moved Mark's body to the back of the pickup truck and called the sheriff.

When the sheriff arrived they told him it was an off roading accident. He accepted that and had the coroner take Mark's body away.

"I'll call Mark's parents and explain what happened when we get to Dr. Jefferson's house" Dr. Thomas said sadly.

Jonathan told him to tell Mark's parents that we would take call of all the funeral expenses and anything else them needed.

"Remember in order to avoid all of us being put in the looney bin, we have to stick to the off roading story" Dr. Thomas said looking sternly at Shelly.

"Ok" she said weakly.

The doctors helped David prepare his great grandmother's remains for his trip home. He asked if there was anything he could do to help with what was happening here, but they assured him that he should go and take care of his great grandmother. All will be well here.

I told him that he was always welcome here and to come back to visit anytime, but wait until we have finished our work here first. He wholeheartedly agreed.

Chapter 14

After David left we decided to go back to Dr. Jefferson's house to rest, eat and regroup. Nora was like a mother hen tending to our wounds, feeding us and making sure we were all taken care of.

Morning came to quickly it seemed to me. As we all prepared for another battle I told everybody how much I appreciated their help and we all expressed sorrow on losing Mark. With determination in my heart we all headed back to our house.

The day was strange. It was cold, the sky was overcast with a slight wind blowing, but what was really strange about it was that it was quiet. No birds singing, no dogs barking, no noise from the wind. Nothing.

Cautiously we went up onto the veranda, expecting something to happen, nothing did. Tension was building when Jonathan opened the front door. We were met with the most horrid stench you could imagine. There was a heaving mist covering the floors, it was so cold that you could see your breath. It too was quiet, too quiet. Jonathan was the first to speak.

"I am Jonathan Chamberlain. This is my house. I am not going to be scared out by you no matter what you do. So you might as well get used to the fact that I am going to get rid of you one way or the other".

A white flash streaked down the staircase and knocked me flat on my ass.

"What did I do? I didn't say anything" I said brushing my butt off as I got up just to find out that the floor was all gooey.

"Yuck, what the hell is this stuff".

"I guess you've been slimed" Vince said smiling.

"Who do you think that was that knocked Amy down, Doc?" Natasha asked.

"Well we know who it wasn't by process of elimination. That leaves us with two that I can think of. It could be either Angela or Constance".

"I didn't do anything to either of them, why pick on me?" I asked.

"Jonathan looks like Nathaniel, doesn't he?"

"Yes, but . . ."

"Maybe they see you as one of Nathaniel's ladies and they want to hurt you as they were hurt".

I started to speak just as my face was slapped by an invisible hand.

"Hey, cut that out!" I yelled.

"Vince, Natasha take Amy out on the veranda before she gets really hurt" Dr. Jefferson said.

"No, I'm not going anywhere. If they want me, I'll fight them. This is my house and no ghost is going to keep me out. Constance, Angela, you husband Nathaniel is dead. I don't want him. He was an evil man and I'm sorry for the hurt he caused you and your children" I called walking into the front parlor. I waited for a response, but nothing happened.

Father O'Malley went from room to room in the house

staring from upstairs working down saying blessings without any incidents.

"I think that we may have cleared the house" he said coming into the front parlor. The mist had subsided and the gooey stuff on the floor seeped back into the floor boards as he walked in.

"Did you ever find the portal" I asked Jason.

"As a matter of fact I found several cold spots in the house but none that I would consider the "portal" cold spot" he replied.

"Do you wan to stay here tonight to see if the house is cleared" Jonathan asked me.

"We might as well, we will never know if it is clear if we don't. Dr. Jefferson maybe you, Dr. Thomas and the team should go home and leave us here tonight by ourselves to see if anything happens. If anything does happen we will be pounding down your door".

After reassuring everybody we would be ok they all left, leaving me and Jonathan, Vince and Natasha to fend for ourselves. That evening all went well, we enjoyed a nervous but quiet meal and much needed conversation about everything except the house. Every once in a while we would hear a strange noise and all jump ready to run but nothing happened.

When it came time to retire, Natasha told Vince she wanted him in her room for "protection purposes", which being a typical male agreed to, smiling.

All went well for the next week. Vince had to return to teaching at the college and Natasha said she wanted to see what college life was like so they both left smiling all the while in her bright red sports car, top down, of course.

Jonathan and I settled down to what we thought was going to be a normal life here, but I knew deep in my gut that there was still something wrong here and all was not well.

One night after everybody had left we were getting ready for bed. Jonathan was stretched out comfortably on the bed and I was sitting at Angela's dressing table when I saw her image in the mirror standing behind me. I closed my eyes hoping that when I opened them she would be gone. No such luck.

"Jonathan, Angela is in the room with us."

"Don't start that again" he said angrily but as he started to sit up, she pounced on him. I was so scared I couldn't move, all I could do was watch in the mirror what was happening.

She was hitting him and trying to get her hand on his throat. He thrashed about on the bed trying to get her off. Finally I was able to move but all I could grab at was air. I looked over in the mirror and could see him image on him so I yelled to Jonathan which way to defend himself. Unfortunately I was too late she was chocking him and lifting him off the bed.

I had to do something. I remembered what Natasha, Tina and Shelly had said about the lady of the house still residing in the house, so I grabbed a heavy book from the night stand and smashed the mirror of the dressing table. Jonathan fell to the floor with a loud thump, coughing and gasping for breath.

I ran to him making sure he was alright. Helping him stand up and holding onto him, his body went stiff. Without moving I asked "Jonathan what's wrong?" He turned me around as said "Look".

We were looking at a hole in the wall behind the mirror and we could see a ghastly sight, there was a skeleton inside the wall.

Cautiously Jonathan moved the vanity and pulled away some of the wall boards. In checking the remains he found that it was a woman and there was a book, besides the one I though, on the floor next to her. Opening it he was astonished to see that it was the last words that Angela wrote before she died. It read:

"Who ever finds this, please forgive me for I have sinned. My husband was such an evil man that I had to find solace in the arms of another. I also had an addition to arsenic, I knew it was wrong but once I tasted it I thirsted for more. It did wonderous things for me at first then I knew it was changing me but I couldn't stop. It was my idea to take Constance's baby away from her for I feared that once Morgan saw it he would stay with her and I could not allow that. It was me that was poisoning my own sister because I felt Morgan turning away from me. He was the one that was supplying me with my arsenic, he told me that he did not like what I was turning into. Nathaniel sent my children away because I was not a fit mother, I even tried poisoning them. I would have succeeded if it wasn't for the servants. Please forgive me my little ones. Morgan came back to see after being away for a long time, I lusted for him and he for me. Nathaniel caught us and killed Morgan. He locked me in my room with no food or water. I thought I was going to go mad because I couldn't get to my supply of arsenic. He forbade the servants to enter my room, he boarded up the hidden passage way into my room behind my dressing table. I find myself inside the wall, I don't know how I got here. There is little light from where the wall is not completely closed. I can barely see him in the room, but I can hear him. He is telling me to confess my sins and write them in this ledger and once I have done that he will let me out.

I have done what he asked of me. I called to him and banged on the walls to come let me out but he doesn't respond.

I have waited for such a long time and Nathaniel has not come, so I will wait patiently. He will come some day, I pray."

That explained quite a few questions about what was going on in our house. One question still goes unanswered, who destroyed Jonathan's body?

After removing Angela's skeleton and placing in her grave in the cemetery the house was finally at peace.

After that we call in experts to check out the grounds with special ground sensing devices that forensic people us to locate bodies. They checked 100 years around each and every building on the place. We didn't tell them about the stone circle.

The only thing that they did find was an old cemetery that had been covered over in tall grasses and brush. I had a landscaping/gardening company come in and clean it up. What they found was the cemetery where the slaves that had lived and worked on the plantation had been buried. The books and ledgers Jonathan and I found in the barn contained names, ages and dates of death of each of the slaves, one of the books contained a map of the cemetery indicating where each person was laid to rest with the name and date therein.

We contacted the local historical society and donated the land to them with some additional land on either side of it so they could use it as they saw fit. We hoped that by giving all this to them would help anybody who might be trying to locate family members, like David did, a better chance of finding them.

Yes, you might have guessed it, we had a construction company come in and check each and every wall and floor to see if there were any more hidden surprises in the house we should know about.

I was so glad to have a normal house again. Jonathan doesn't remember some of the things that happened to him but that's ok. He seems like nothing happened, the only problem he has is when we go out across the field toward the stone circle he seems to get upset. I'll have to have that place torn down so maybe what ever it is lingering there can either move on or cross over.

I am also glad Natasha and Vince got together. The way they worked together during all of this really was great for them. They have started their own psychic paranormal investigation service.

Jonathan gave David one-fourth of what was in the bank account. David said he would put it to goo use. We received a post card from him the other day saying that he has done lots of research and was using the money to help out some of the families that had family members that worked for Nathaniel.

As for me I can sleep at night without any terrifying dreams while petting my new dog.